DreamWorks

PENGUINS OF MADAGASCAR

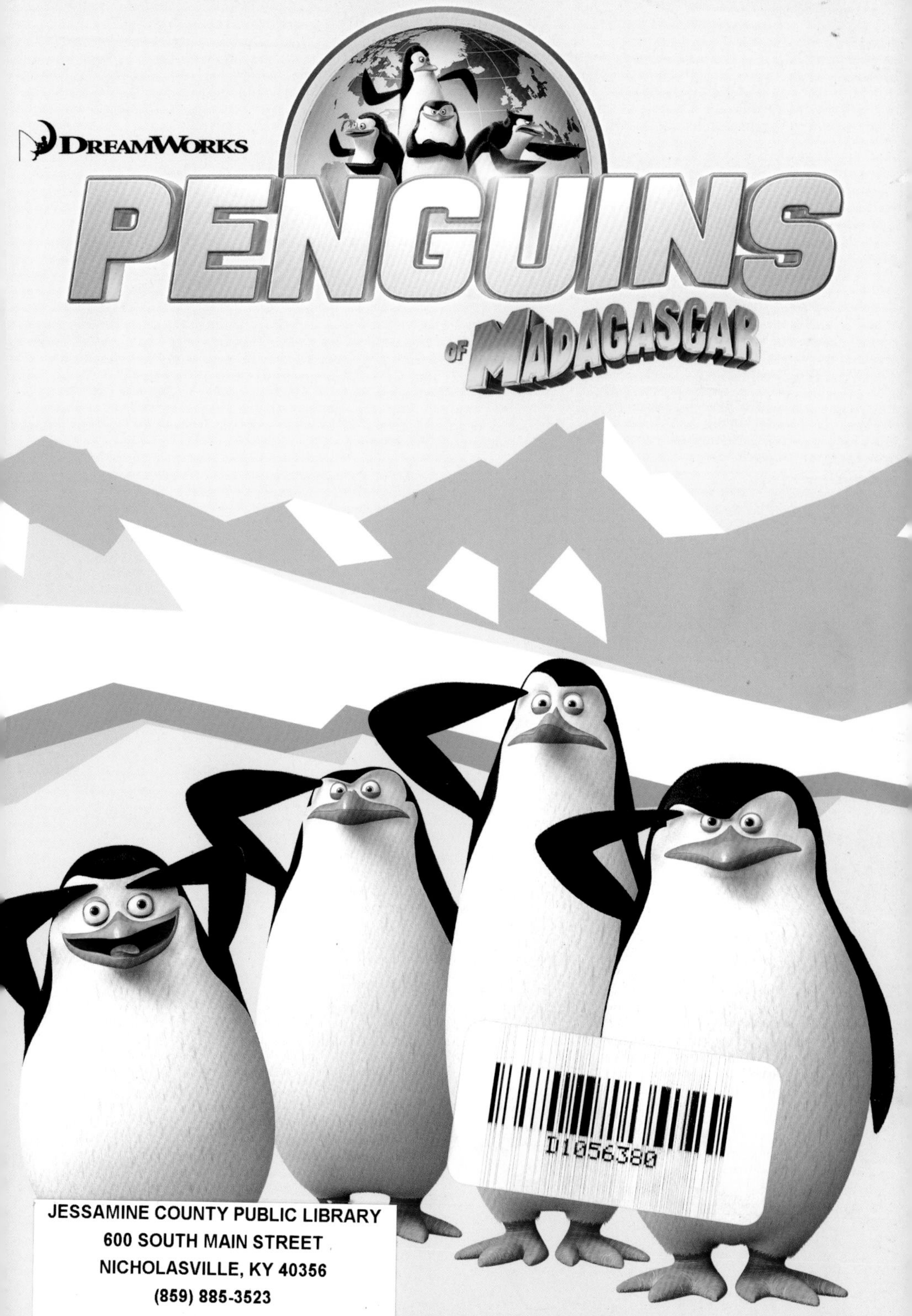

OPERATION: HEIST

THIS BOOK IS BROUGHT TO YOU BY... Senior Editor **Martin Eden**
Production Manager **Obi Onoura**
Production Supervisors **Jackie Flook, Maria Pearson**
Production Assistant **Peter James**
Studio Manager **Emma Smith**
Circulation Manager **Steve Tothill**
Marketing Manager **Ricky Claydon**
Publishing Manager **Darryl Tothill**
Publishing Director **Chris Teather**
Operations Director **Leigh Baulch**
Executive Director **Vivian Cheung**
Publisher **Nick Landau**

ISBN: 9781782762522

10 9 8 7 6 5 4 3 2 1
First printed in China in May 2015.
A CIP catalogue record for this title is available from the British Library.
TCN: 0557

Special thanks to **Corinne Combs, Alyssa Mauney, Barbara Layman.**

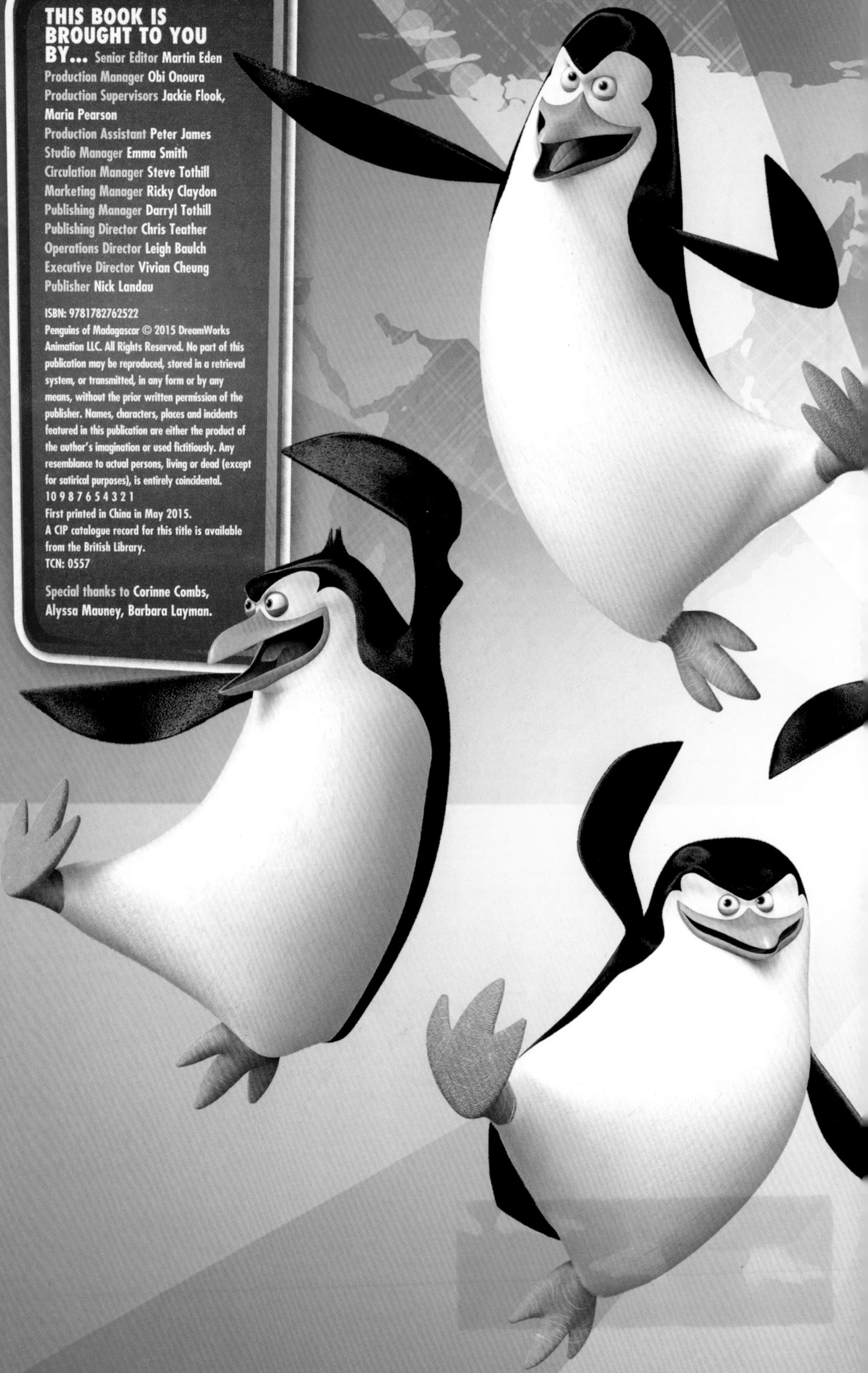

DreamWorks

PENGUINS OF MADAGASCAR

Inside 2 EPIC COMIC STRIPS

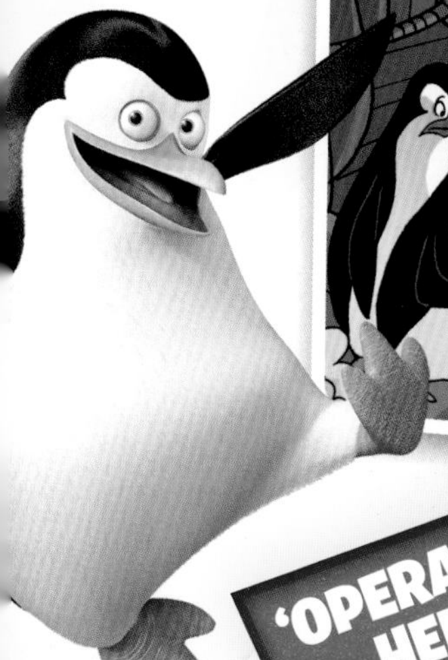

'BIG TOP'

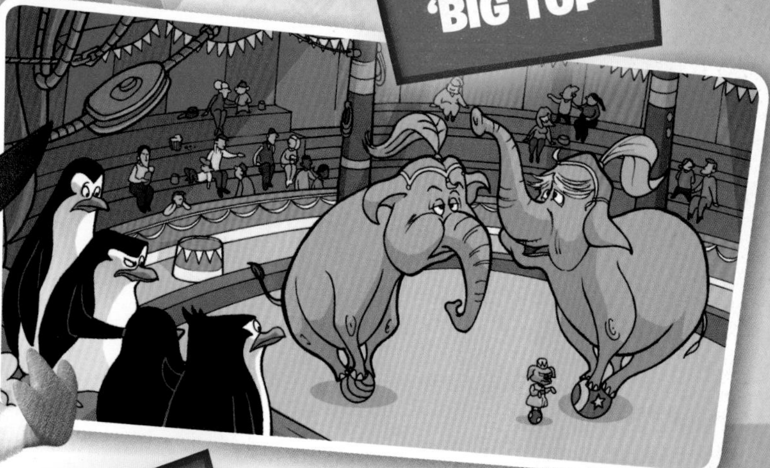

'OPERATION: HEIST'

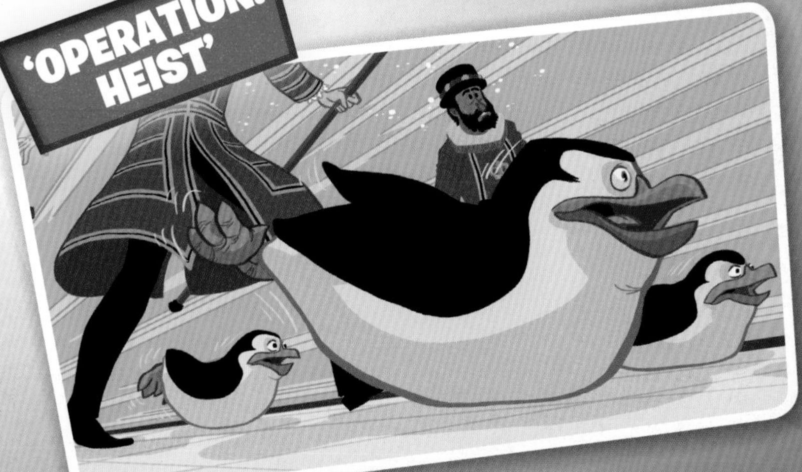

Meet the

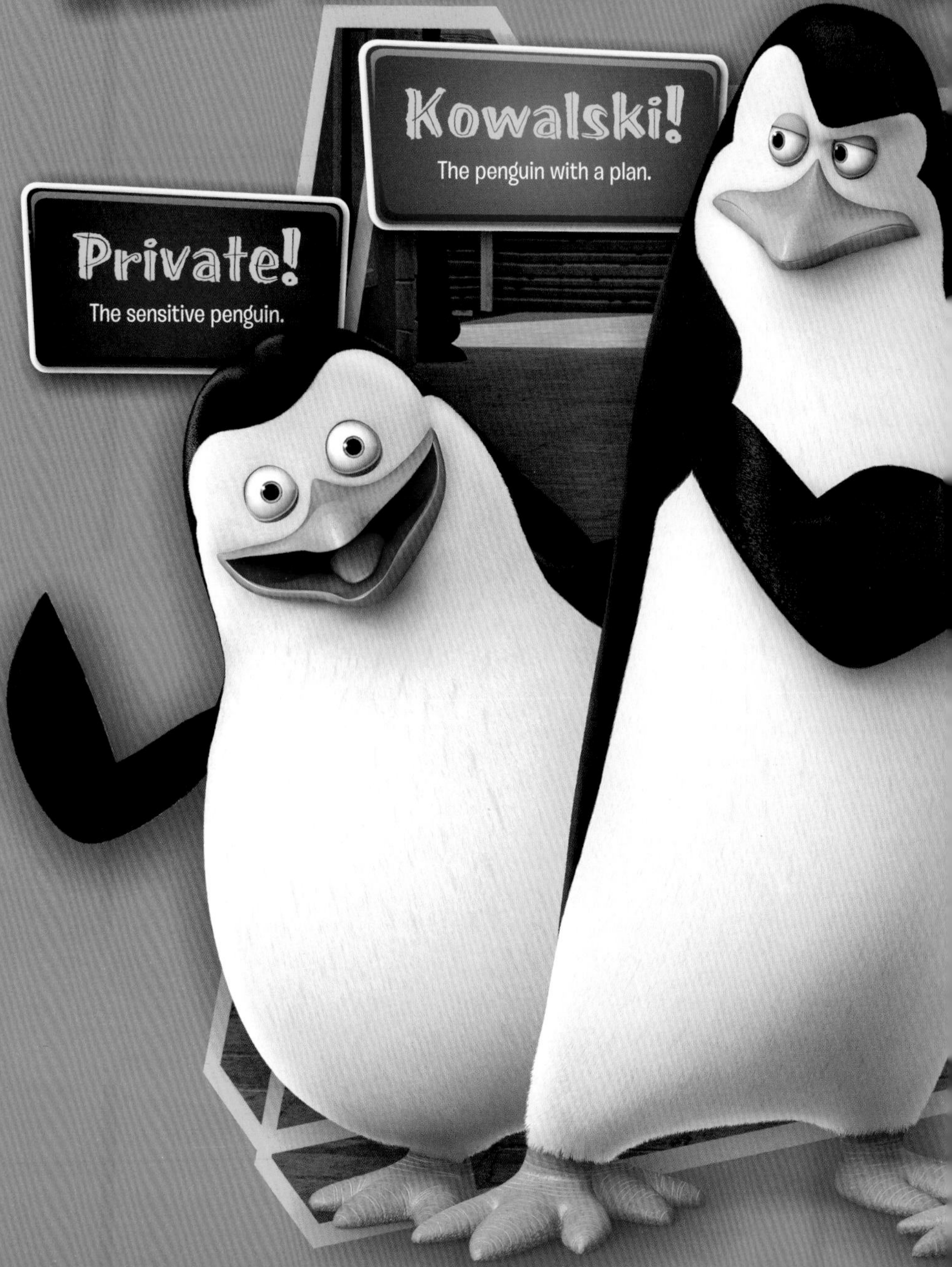
Kowalski!
The penguin with a plan.
Private!
The sensitive penguin.

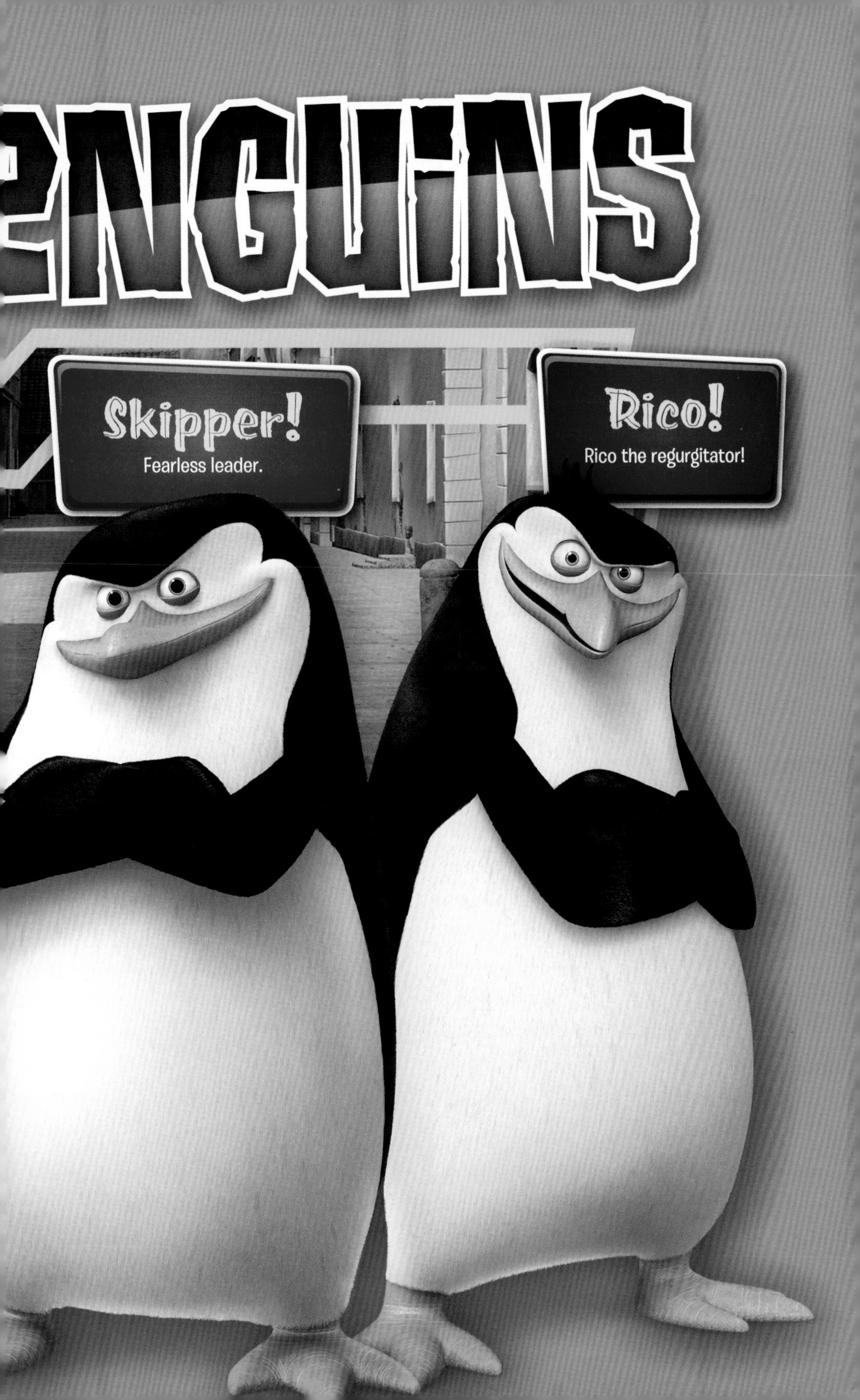
ENGUINS
Skipper!
Fearless leader.
Rico!
Rico the regurgitator!

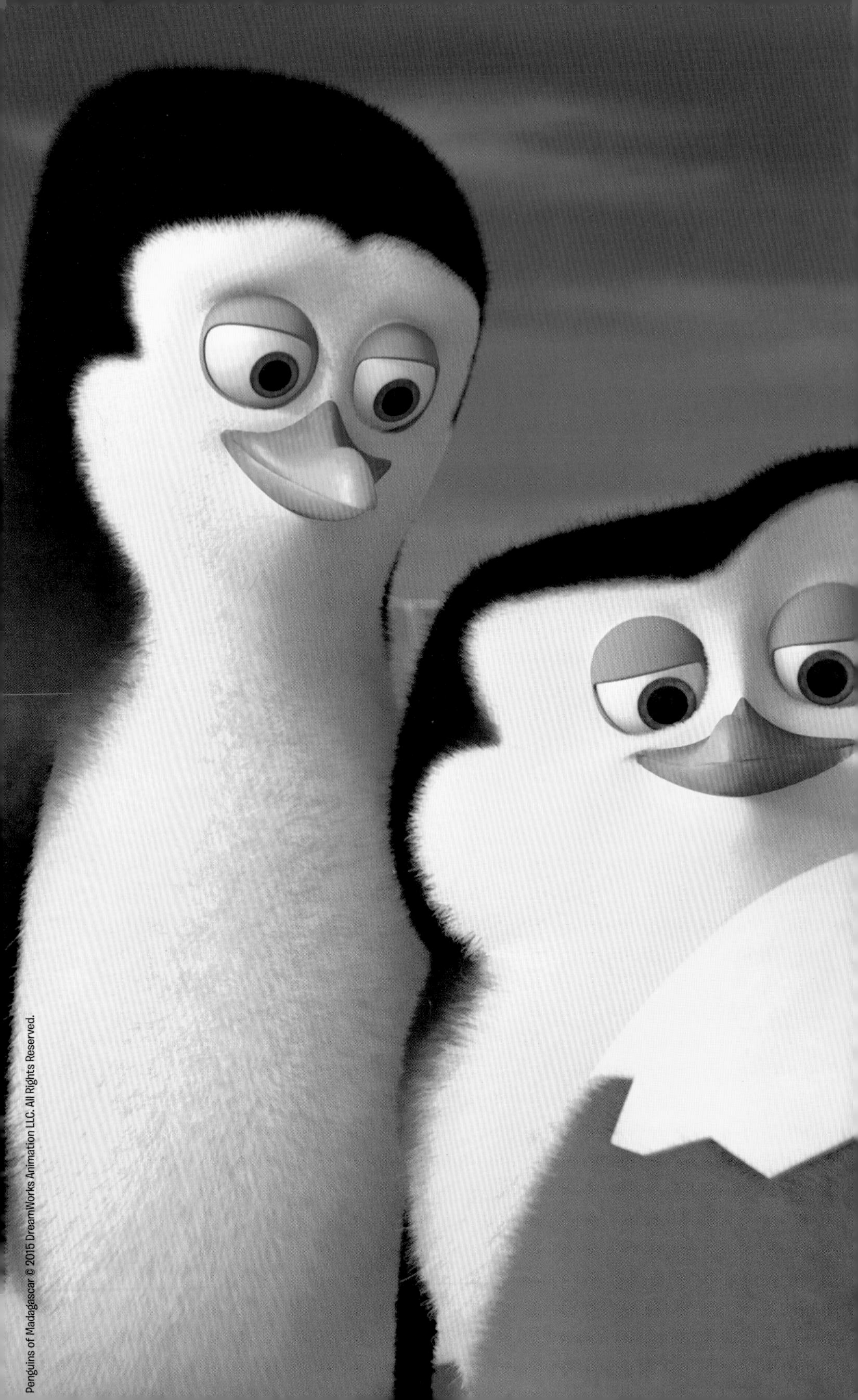

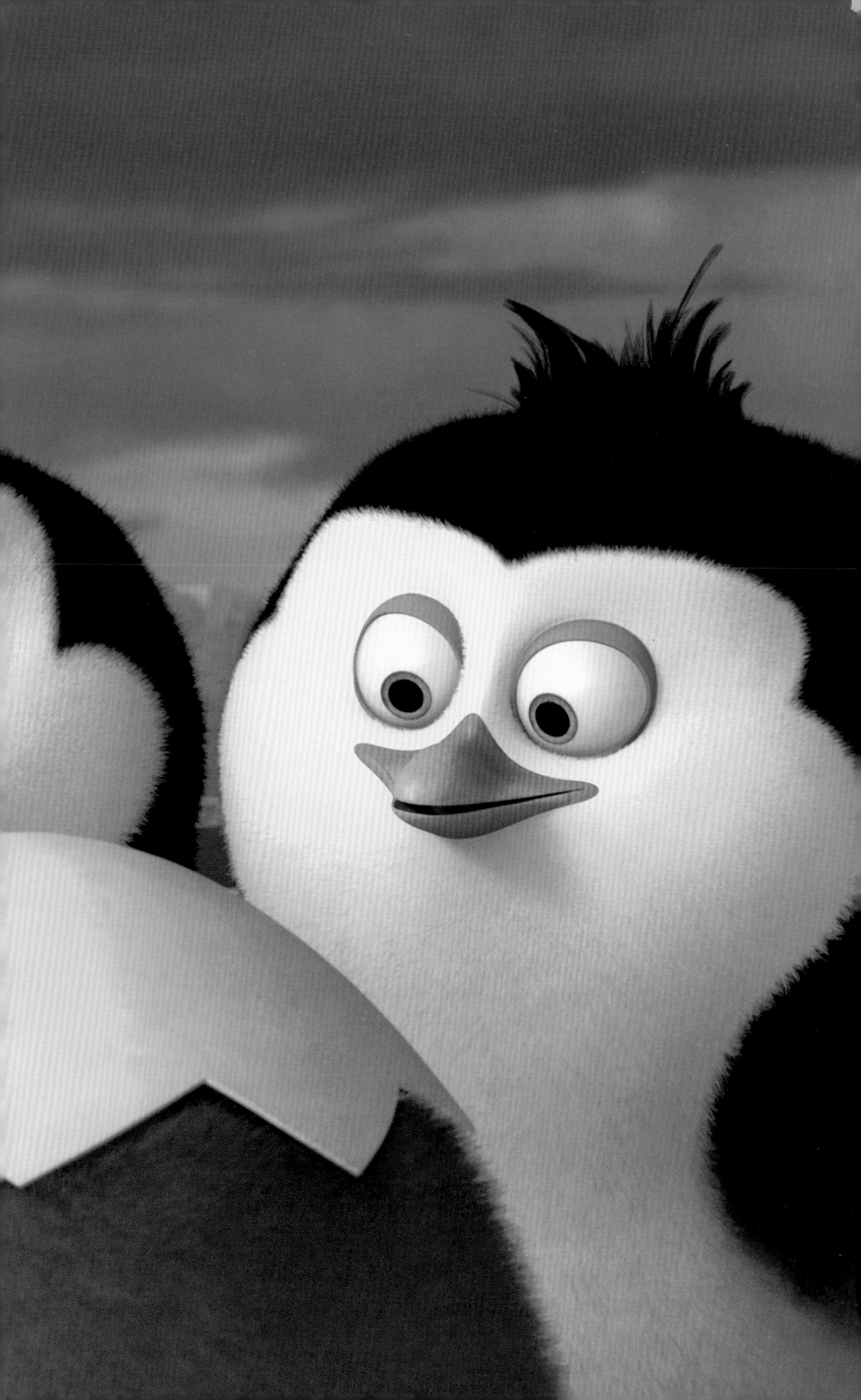

BIG TOP

SCRIPT
Jim Alexander

ART
Egle Bartolini

COLORS
M.L. Sanapo

LETTERING
Jim Campbell

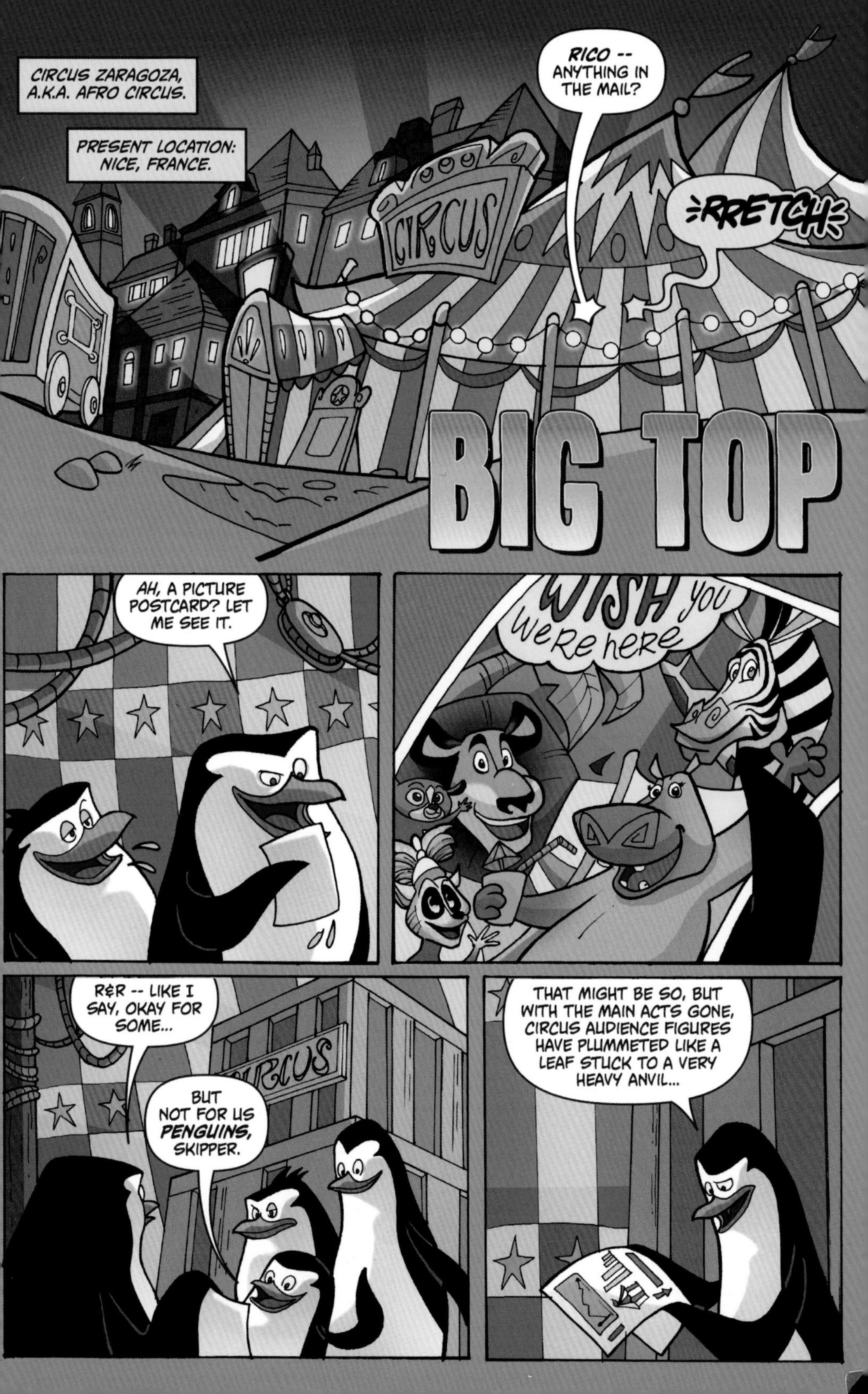
CIRCUS ZARAGOZA, A.K.A. AFRO CIRCUS.
PRESENT LOCATION: NICE, FRANCE.
RICO -- ANYTHING IN THE MAIL?
RRETCH
CIRCUS
BIG TOP
AH, A PICTURE POSTCARD? LET ME SEE IT.
WISH you were here
R&R -- LIKE I SAY, OKAY FOR SOME...
CIRCUS
BUT NOT FOR US PENGUINS, SKIPPER.
THAT MIGHT BE SO, BUT WITH THE MAIN ACTS GONE, CIRCUS AUDIENCE FIGURES HAVE PLUMMETED LIKE A LEAF STUCK TO A VERY HEAVY ANVIL...

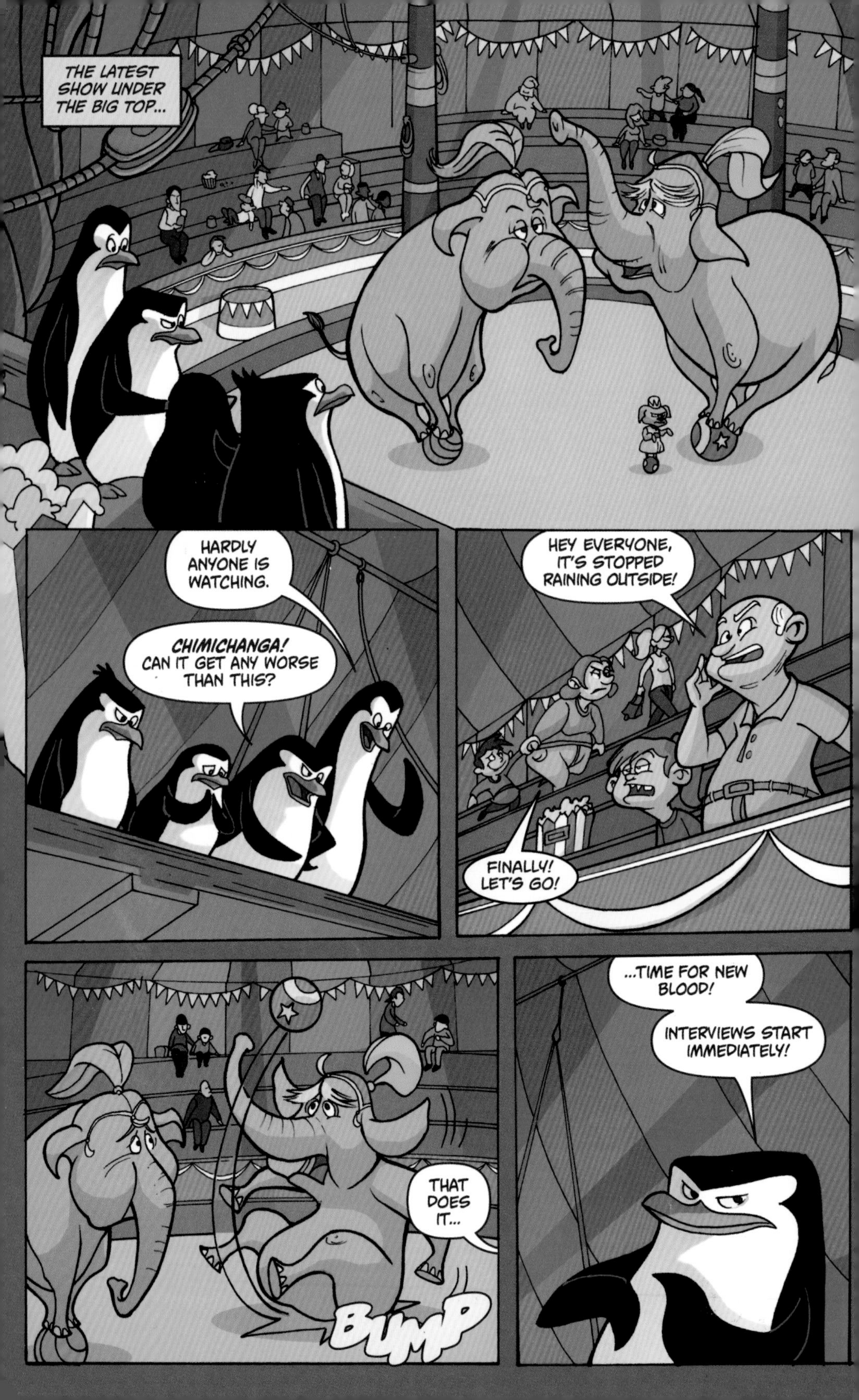
THE LATEST SHOW UNDER THE BIG TOP...
HARDLY ANYONE IS WATCHING.
CHIMICHANGA! CAN IT GET ANY WORSE THAN THIS?
HEY EVERYONE, IT'S STOPPED RAINING OUTSIDE!
FINALLY! LET'S GO!
THAT DOES IT...
BUMP
...TIME FOR NEW BLOOD!
INTERVIEWS START IMMEDIATELY!

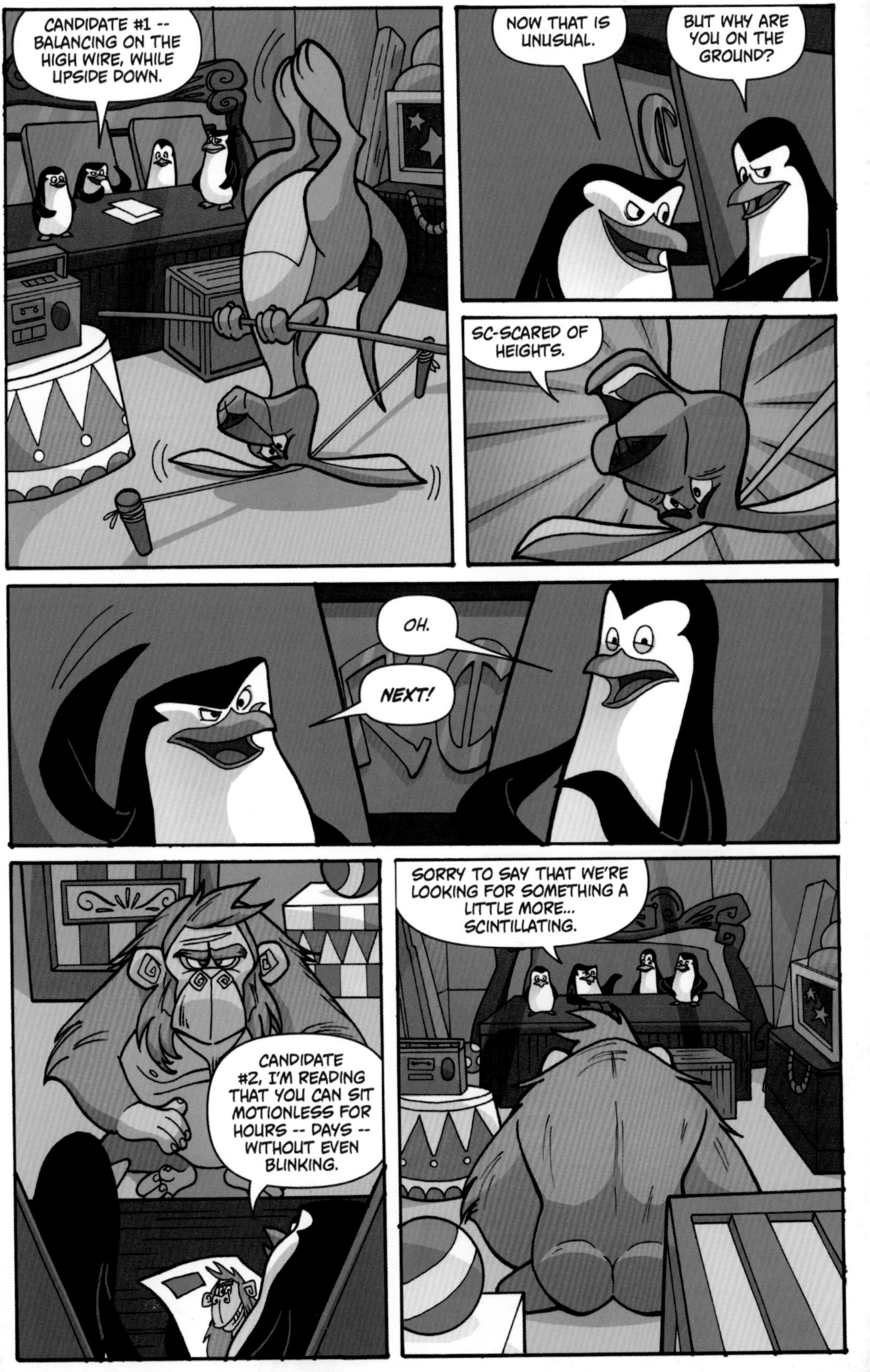
CANDIDATE #1 -- BALANCING ON THE HIGH WIRE, WHILE UPSIDE DOWN.
NOW THAT IS UNUSUAL.
BUT WHY ARE YOU ON THE GROUND?
SC-SCARED OF HEIGHTS.
OH.
NEXT!
CANDIDATE #2, I'M READING THAT YOU CAN SIT MOTIONLESS FOR HOURS -- DAYS -- WITHOUT EVEN BLINKING.
SORRY TO SAY THAT WE'RE LOOKING FOR SOMETHING A LITTLE MORE... SCINTILLATING.

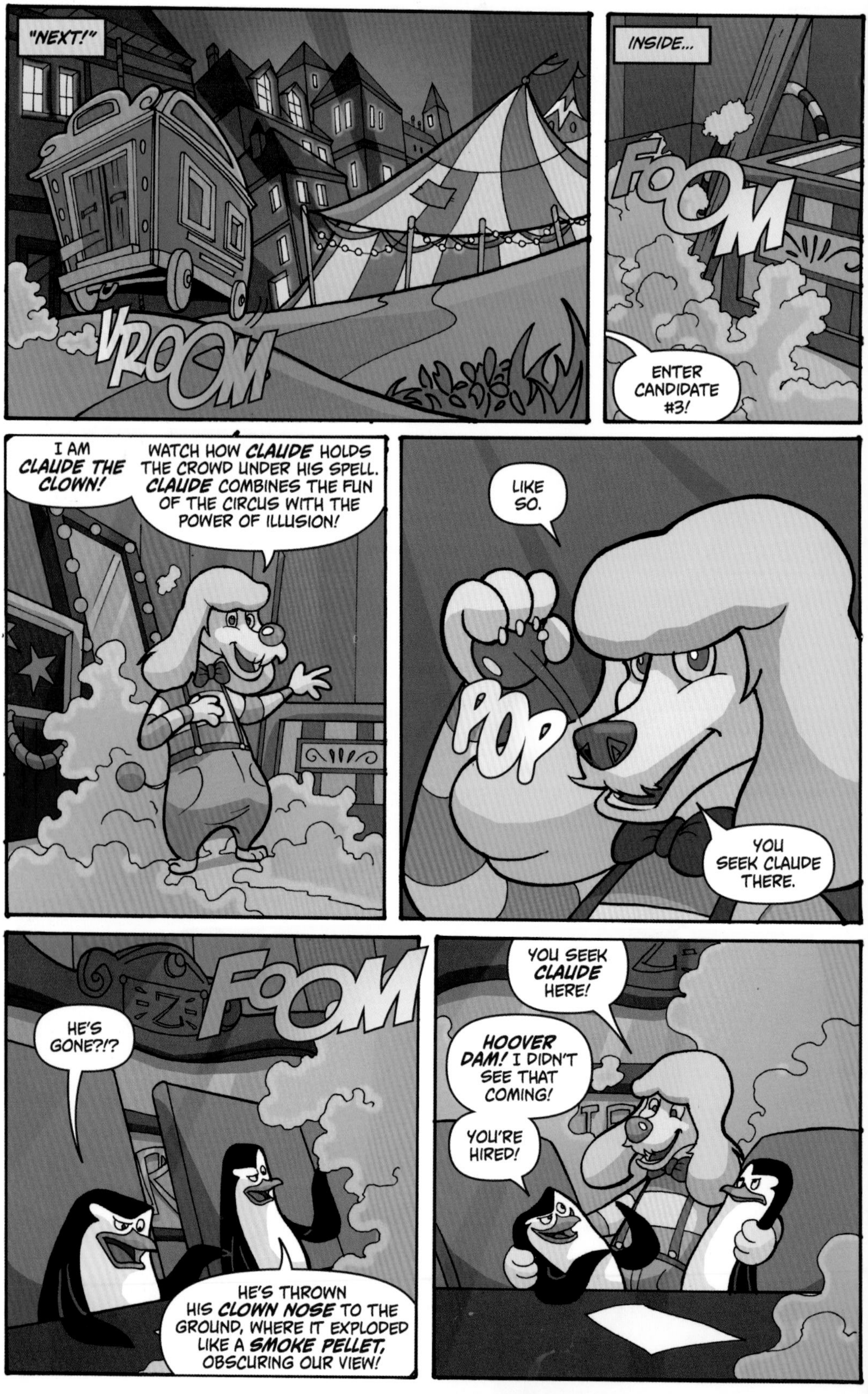
"NEXT!"
VROOM
INSIDE...
FOOM
ENTER CANDIDATE #3!
I AM CLAUDE THE CLOWN!
WATCH HOW CLAUDE HOLDS THE CROWD UNDER HIS SPELL. CLAUDE COMBINES THE FUN OF THE CIRCUS WITH THE POWER OF ILLUSION!
LIKE SO.
POP
YOU SEEK CLAUDE THERE.
FOOM
HE'S GONE?!?
HE'S THROWN HIS CLOWN NOSE TO THE GROUND, WHERE IT EXPLODED LIKE A SMOKE PELLET, OBSCURING OUR VIEW!
YOU SEEK CLAUDE HERE!
HOOVER DAM! I DIDN'T SEE THAT COMING!
YOU'RE HIRED!

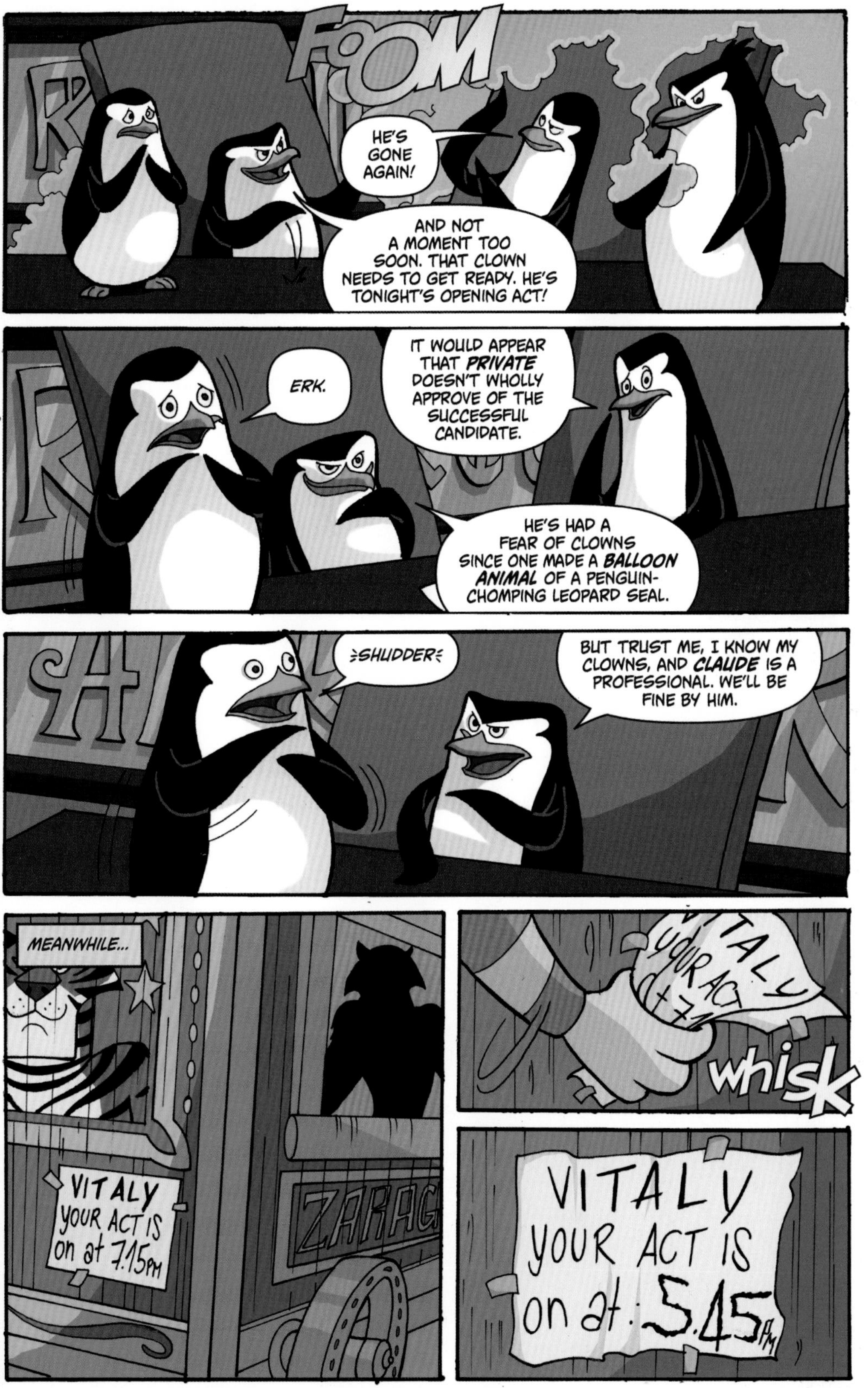
FOOM
HE'S GONE AGAIN!
AND NOT A MOMENT TOO SOON. THAT CLOWN NEEDS TO GET READY. HE'S TONIGHT'S OPENING ACT!
ERK.
IT WOULD APPEAR THAT *PRIVATE* DOESN'T WHOLLY APPROVE OF THE SUCCESSFUL CANDIDATE.
HE'S HAD A FEAR OF CLOWNS SINCE ONE MADE A *BALLOON ANIMAL* OF A PENGUIN-CHOMPING LEOPARD SEAL.
SHUDDER
BUT TRUST ME, I KNOW MY CLOWNS, AND *CLAUDE* IS A PROFESSIONAL. WE'LL BE FINE BY HIM.
MEANWHILE...
VITALY YOUR ACT IS on at 7.15PM
whisk
VITALY YOUR ACT IS on at 5.45PM

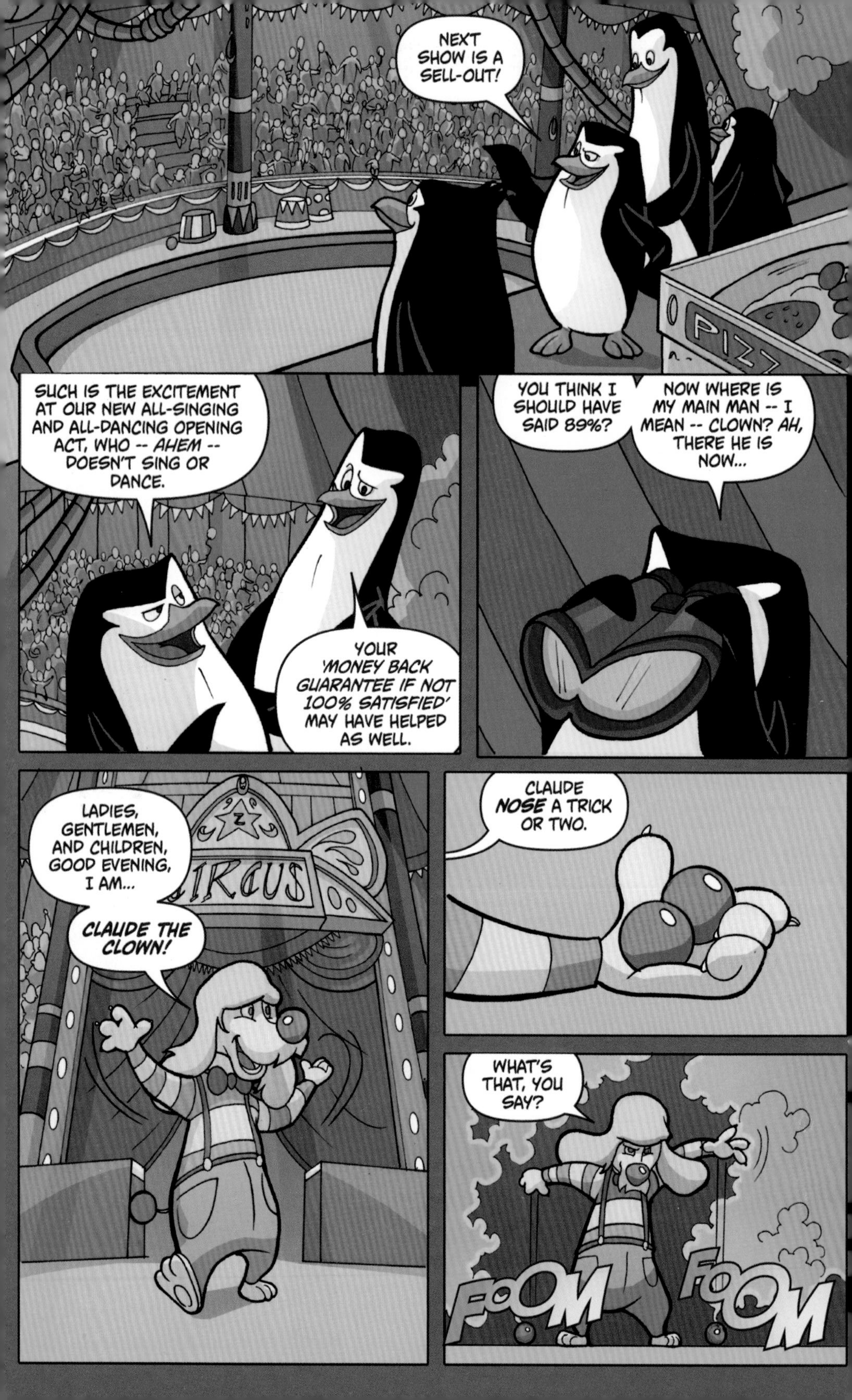
NEXT SHOW IS A SELL-OUT!
SUCH IS THE EXCITEMENT AT OUR NEW ALL-SINGING AND ALL-DANCING OPENING ACT, WHO -- *AHEM* -- DOESN'T SING OR DANCE.
YOUR *'MONEY BACK GUARANTEE IF NOT 100% SATISFIED'* MAY HAVE HELPED AS WELL.
YOU THINK I SHOULD HAVE SAID 89%?
NOW WHERE IS MY MAIN MAN -- I MEAN -- CLOWN? AH, THERE HE IS NOW...
LADIES, GENTLEMEN, AND CHILDREN, GOOD EVENING, I AM...
CLAUDE THE CLOWN!
CLAUDE ***NOSE*** A TRICK OR TWO.
WHAT'S THAT, YOU SAY?
FOOM
FOOM

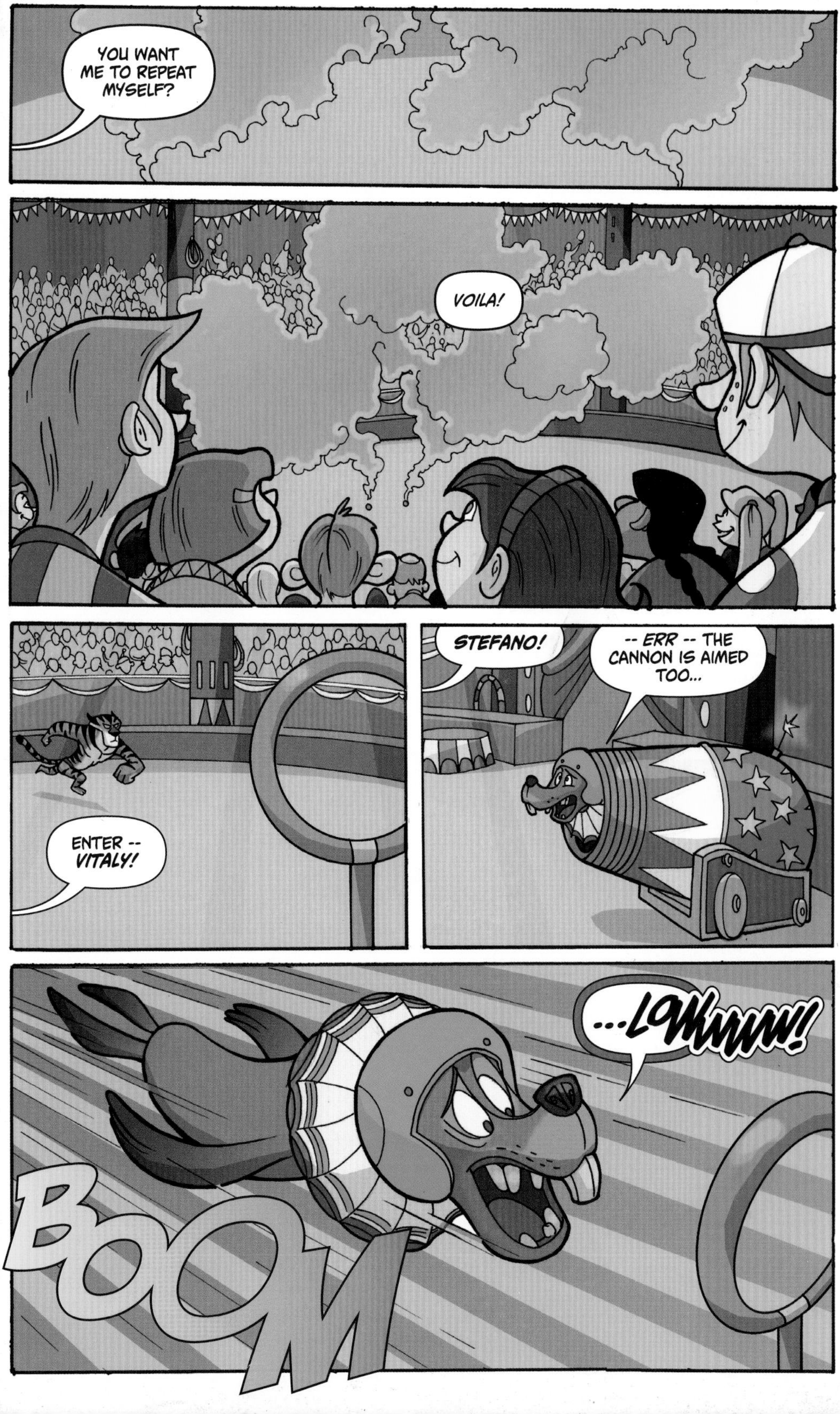
YOU WANT ME TO REPEAT MYSELF?
VOILA!
ENTER -- VITALY!
STEFANO!
-- ERR -- THE CANNON IS AIMED TOO...
...LOWWWW!
BOOM

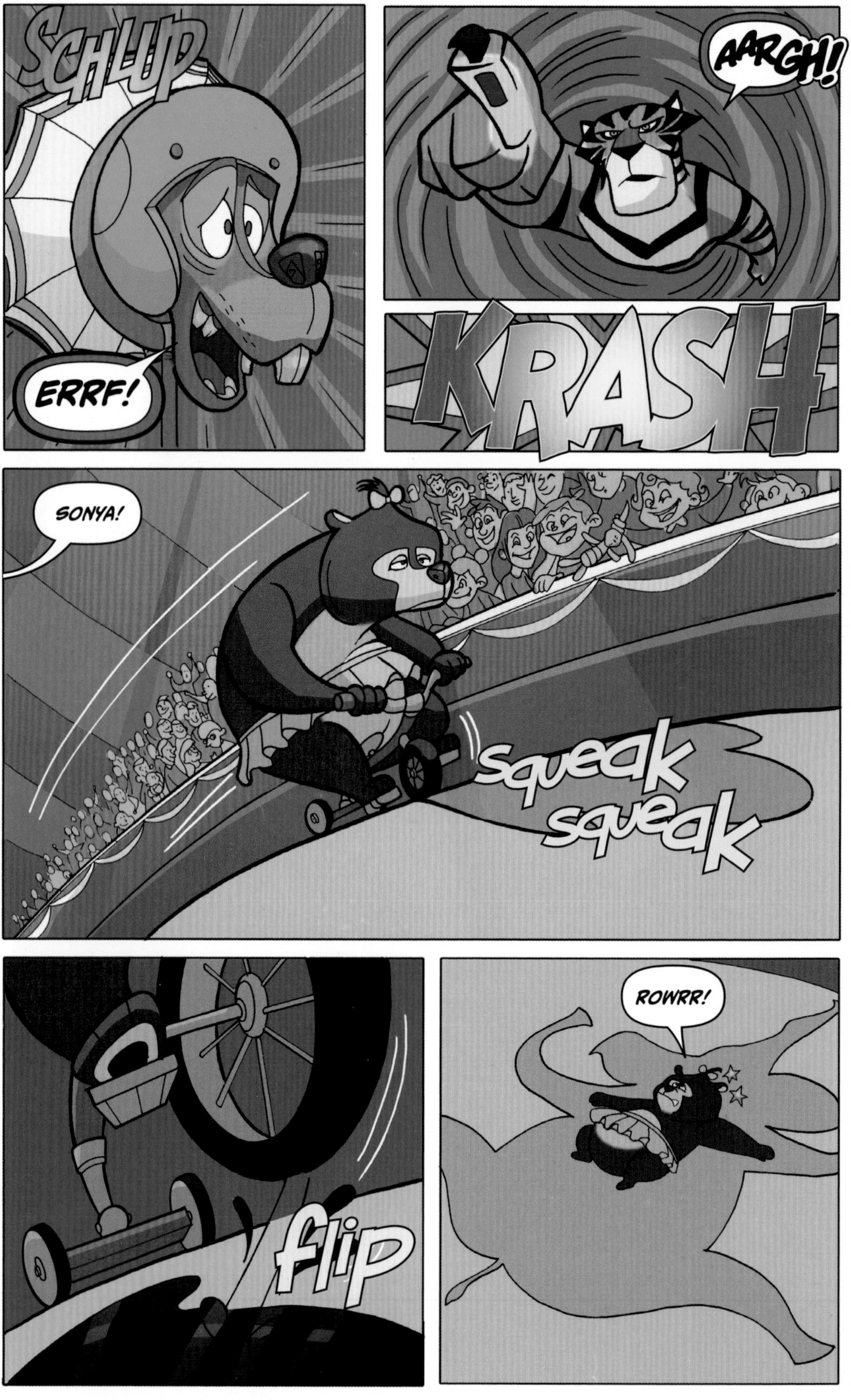
SCHLUP
ERRF!
AARGH!
KRASH
SONYA!
squeak
squeak
flip
ROWRR!

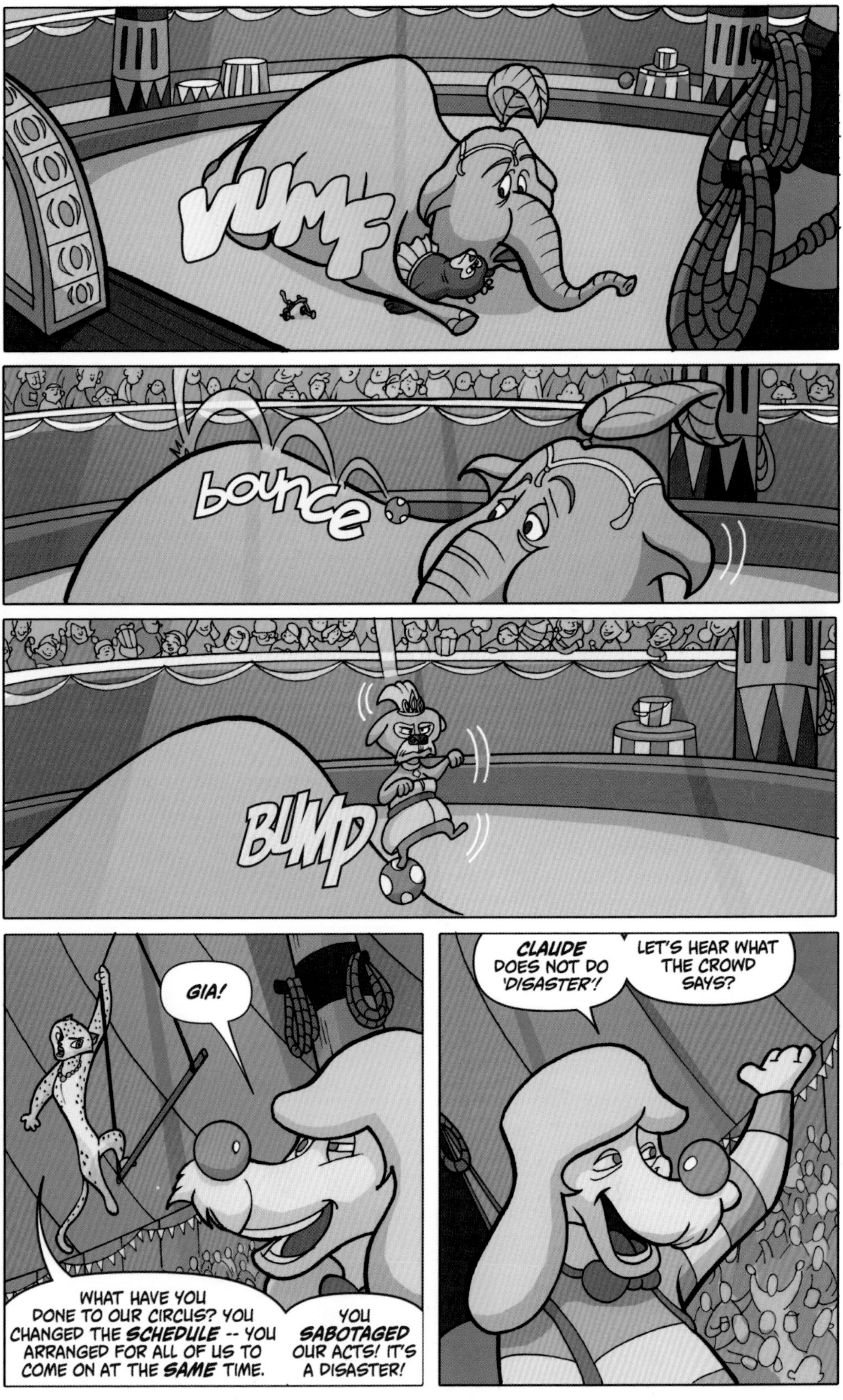
VUMF
bounce
BUMP
GIA!
WHAT HAVE YOU DONE TO OUR CIRCUS? YOU CHANGED THE SCHEDULE -- YOU ARRANGED FOR ALL OF US TO COME ON AT THE SAME TIME.
YOU SABOTAGED OUR ACTS! IT'S A DISASTER!
CLAUDE DOES NOT DO 'DISASTER'!
LET'S HEAR WHAT THE CROWD SAYS?

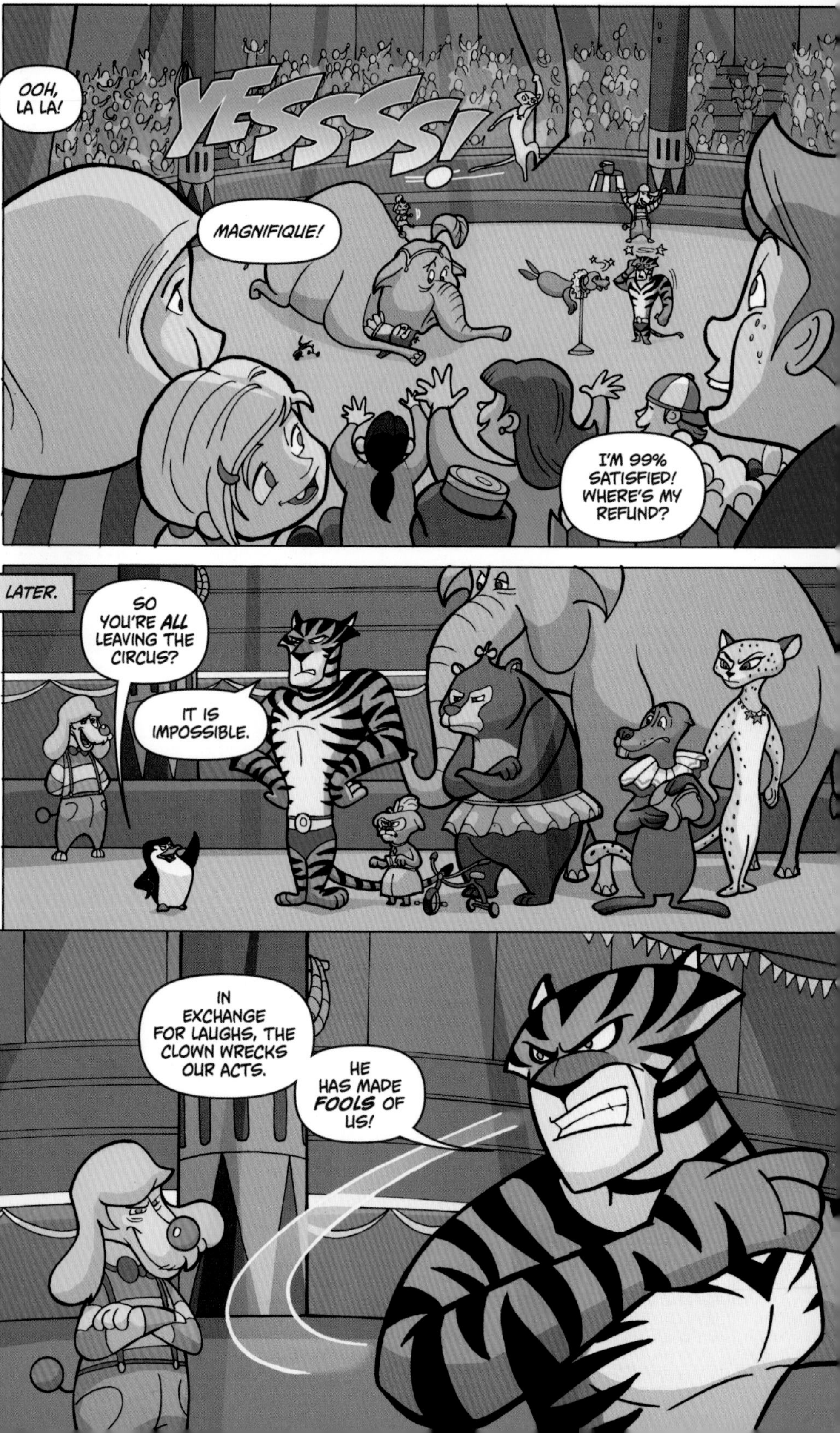
OOH, LA LA!
YESSSS!
MAGNIFIQUE!
I'M 99% SATISFIED! WHERE'S MY REFUND?
LATER.
SO YOU'RE ALL LEAVING THE CIRCUS?
IT IS IMPOSSIBLE.
IN EXCHANGE FOR LAUGHS, THE CLOWN WRECKS OUR ACTS.
HE HAS MADE FOOLS OF US!

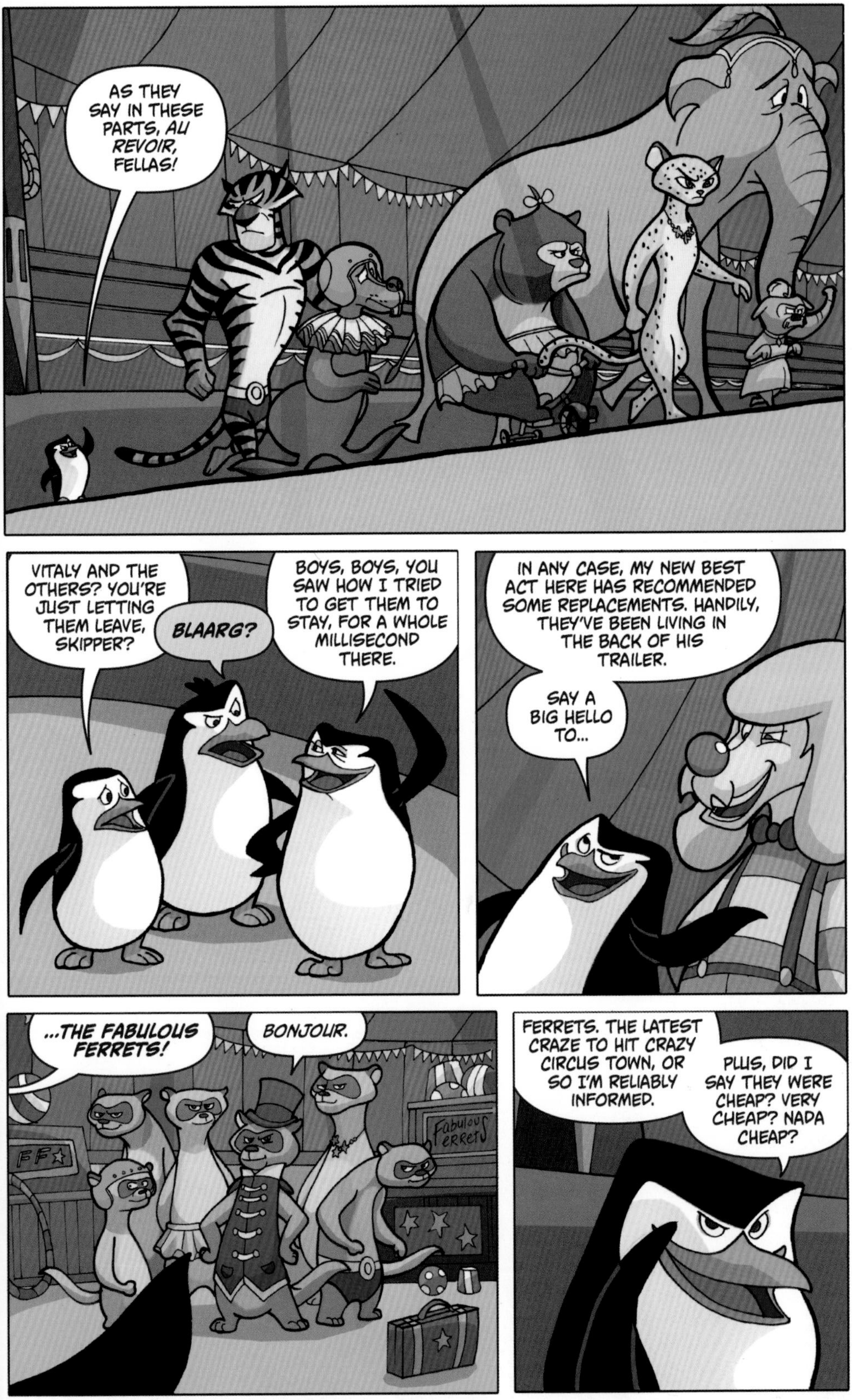
AS THEY SAY IN THESE PARTS, *AU REVOIR,* FELLAS!
VITALY AND THE OTHERS? YOU'RE JUST LETTING THEM LEAVE, SKIPPER?
BLAARG?
BOYS, BOYS, YOU SAW HOW I TRIED TO GET THEM TO STAY, FOR A WHOLE MILLISECOND THERE.
IN ANY CASE, MY NEW BEST ACT HERE HAS RECOMMENDED SOME REPLACEMENTS. HANDILY, THEY'VE BEEN LIVING IN THE BACK OF HIS TRAILER.
SAY A BIG HELLO TO...
...THE FABULOUS FERRETS!
BONJOUR.
FF
Fabulous Ferrets
FERRETS. THE LATEST CRAZE TO HIT CRAZY CIRCUS TOWN, OR SO I'M RELIABLY INFORMED.
PLUS, DID I SAY THEY WERE CHEAP? VERY CHEAP? NADA CHEAP?

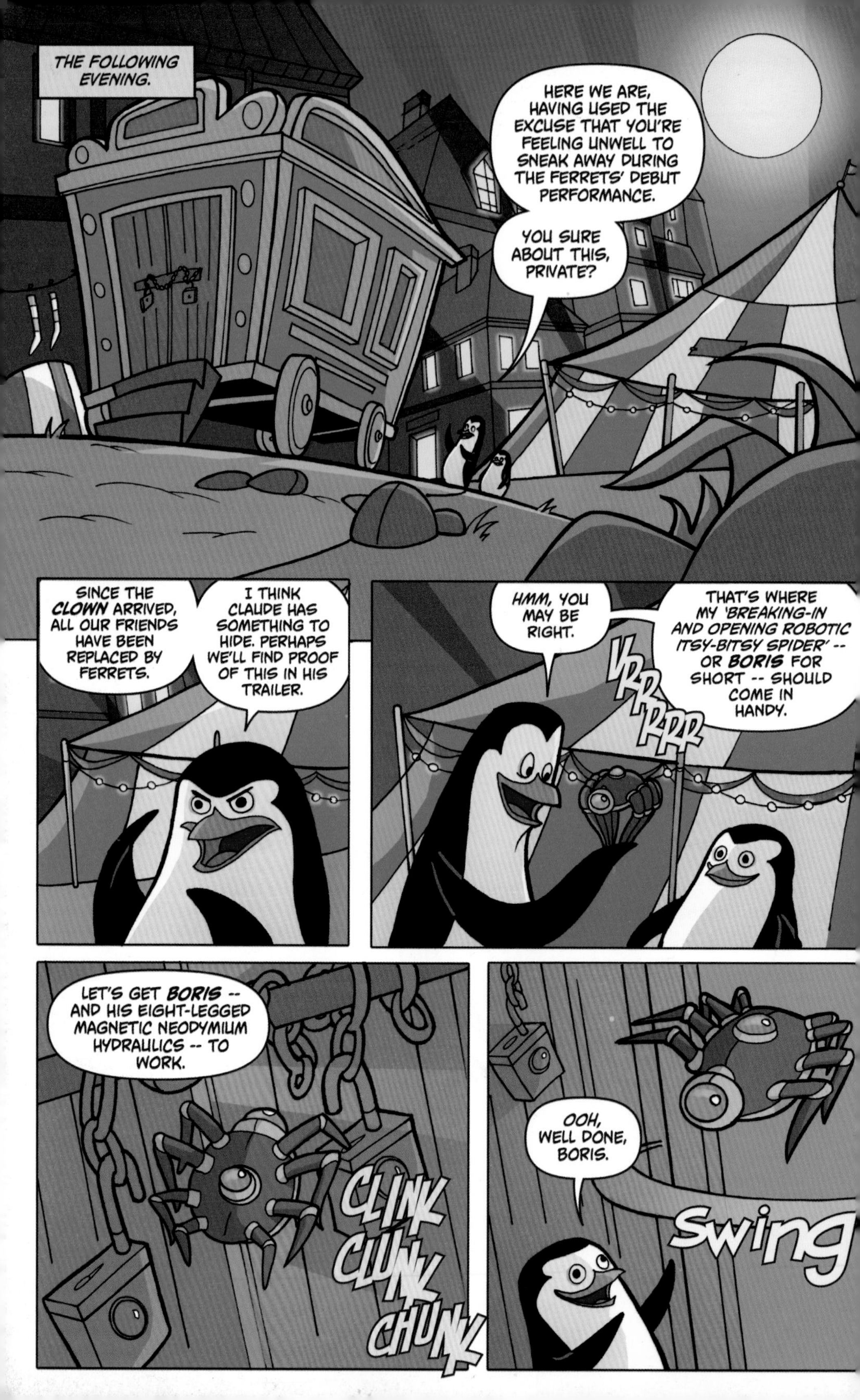
THE FOLLOWING EVENING.
HERE WE ARE, HAVING USED THE EXCUSE THAT YOU'RE FEELING UNWELL TO SNEAK AWAY DURING THE FERRETS' DEBUT PERFORMANCE.
YOU SURE ABOUT THIS, PRIVATE?
SINCE THE CLOWN ARRIVED, ALL OUR FRIENDS HAVE BEEN REPLACED BY FERRETS.
I THINK CLAUDE HAS SOMETHING TO HIDE. PERHAPS WE'LL FIND PROOF OF THIS IN HIS TRAILER.
HMM, YOU MAY BE RIGHT.
THAT'S WHERE MY 'BREAKING-IN AND OPENING ROBOTIC ITSY-BITSY SPIDER' -- OR BORIS FOR SHORT -- SHOULD COME IN HANDY.
VRRRRRR
LET'S GET BORIS -- AND HIS EIGHT-LEGGED MAGNETIC NEODYMIUM HYDRAULICS -- TO WORK.
CLINK
CLUNK
CHUNK
OOH, WELL DONE, BORIS.
swing

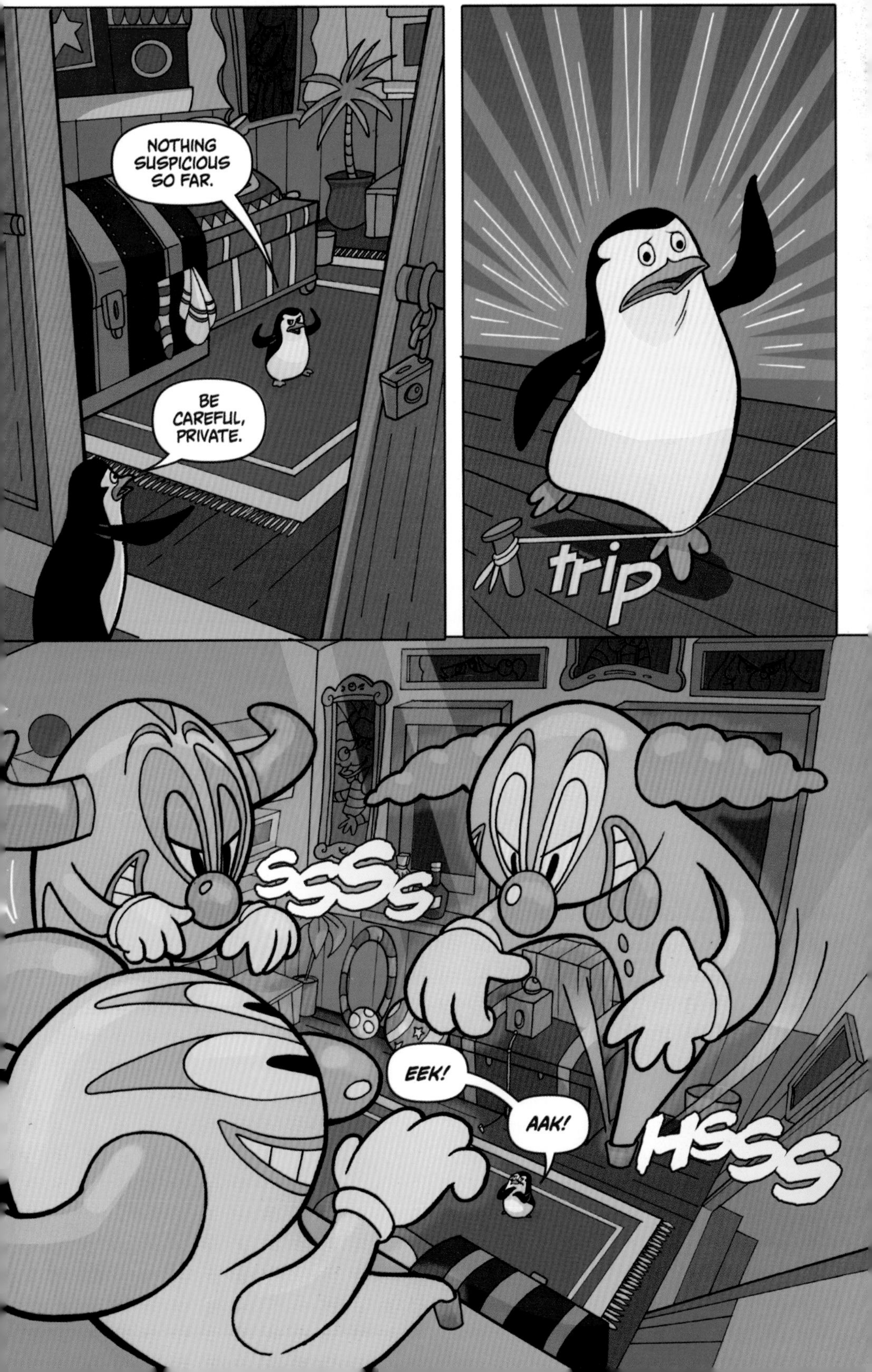
NOTHING SUSPICIOUS SO FAR.
BE CAREFUL, PRIVATE.
trip
SSSS
EEK!
AAK!
HSSS

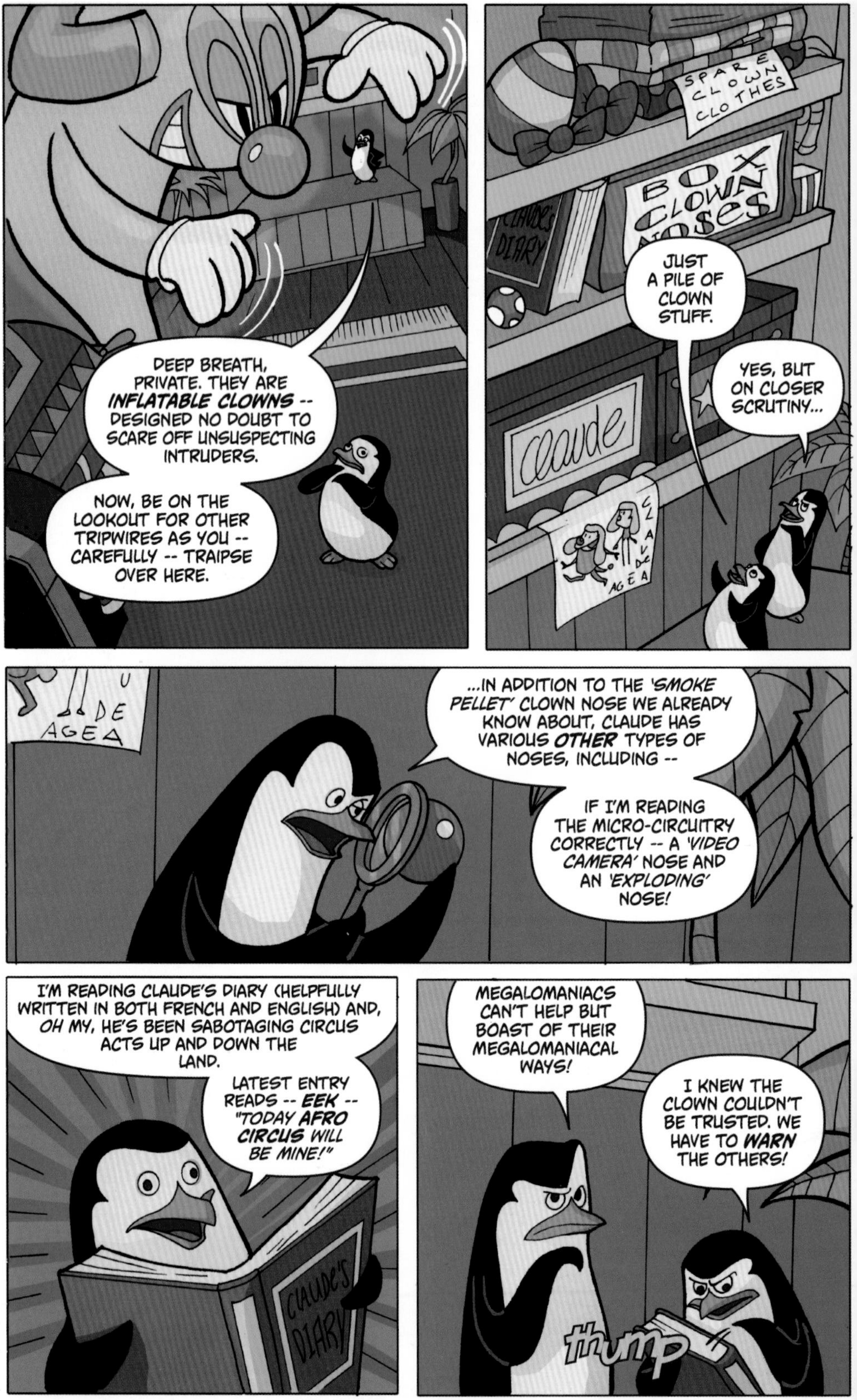
DEEP BREATH, PRIVATE. THEY ARE *INFLATABLE CLOWNS* -- DESIGNED NO DOUBT TO SCARE OFF UNSUSPECTING INTRUDERS.
NOW, BE ON THE LOOKOUT FOR OTHER TRIPWIRES AS YOU -- CAREFULLY -- TRAIPSE OVER HERE.
SPARE CLOWN CLOTHES
BOX X CLOWN NOSES
CLAUDE'S DIARY
JUST A PILE OF CLOWN STUFF.
YES, BUT ON CLOSER SCRUTINY...
CLAUDE
...IN ADDITION TO THE *'SMOKE PELLET'* CLOWN NOSE WE ALREADY KNOW ABOUT, CLAUDE HAS VARIOUS ***OTHER*** TYPES OF NOSES, INCLUDING --
IF I'M READING THE MICRO-CIRCUITRY CORRECTLY -- A *'VIDEO CAMERA'* NOSE AND AN *'EXPLODING'* NOSE!
I'M READING CLAUDE'S DIARY (HELPFULLY WRITTEN IN BOTH FRENCH AND ENGLISH) AND, *OH MY,* HE'S BEEN SABOTAGING CIRCUS ACTS UP AND DOWN THE LAND.
LATEST ENTRY READS -- ***EEK*** -- *"TODAY* ***AFRO CIRCUS*** *WILL BE MINE!"*
CLAUDE'S DIARY
MEGALOMANIACS CAN'T HELP BUT BOAST OF THEIR MEGALOMANIACAL WAYS!
I KNEW THE CLOWN COULDN'T BE TRUSTED. WE HAVE TO ***WARN*** THE OTHERS!
thump

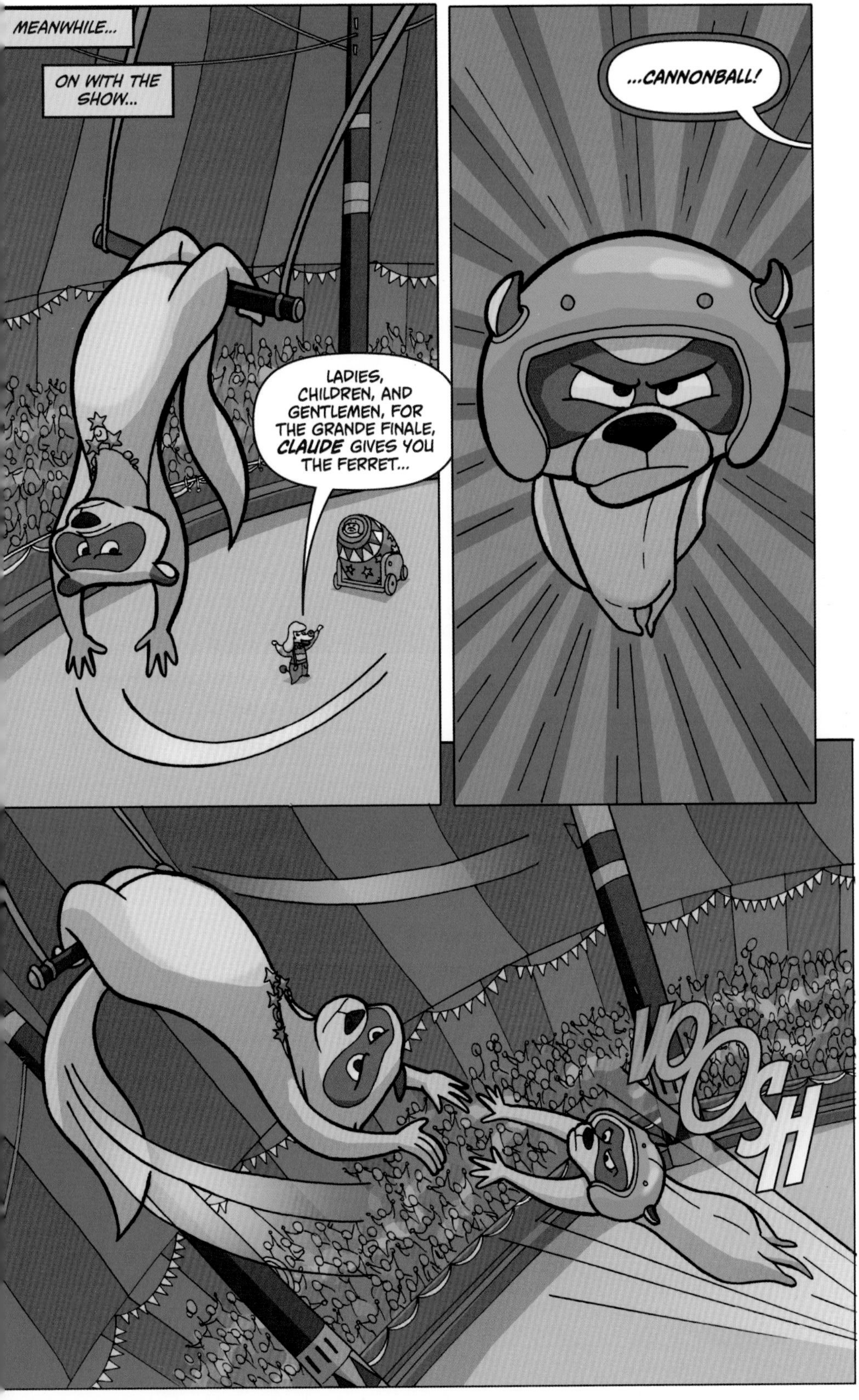
MEANWHILE...
ON WITH THE SHOW...
LADIES, CHILDREN, AND GENTLEMEN, FOR THE GRANDE FINALE, CLAUDE GIVES YOU THE FERRET...
...CANNONBALL!
WOOSH

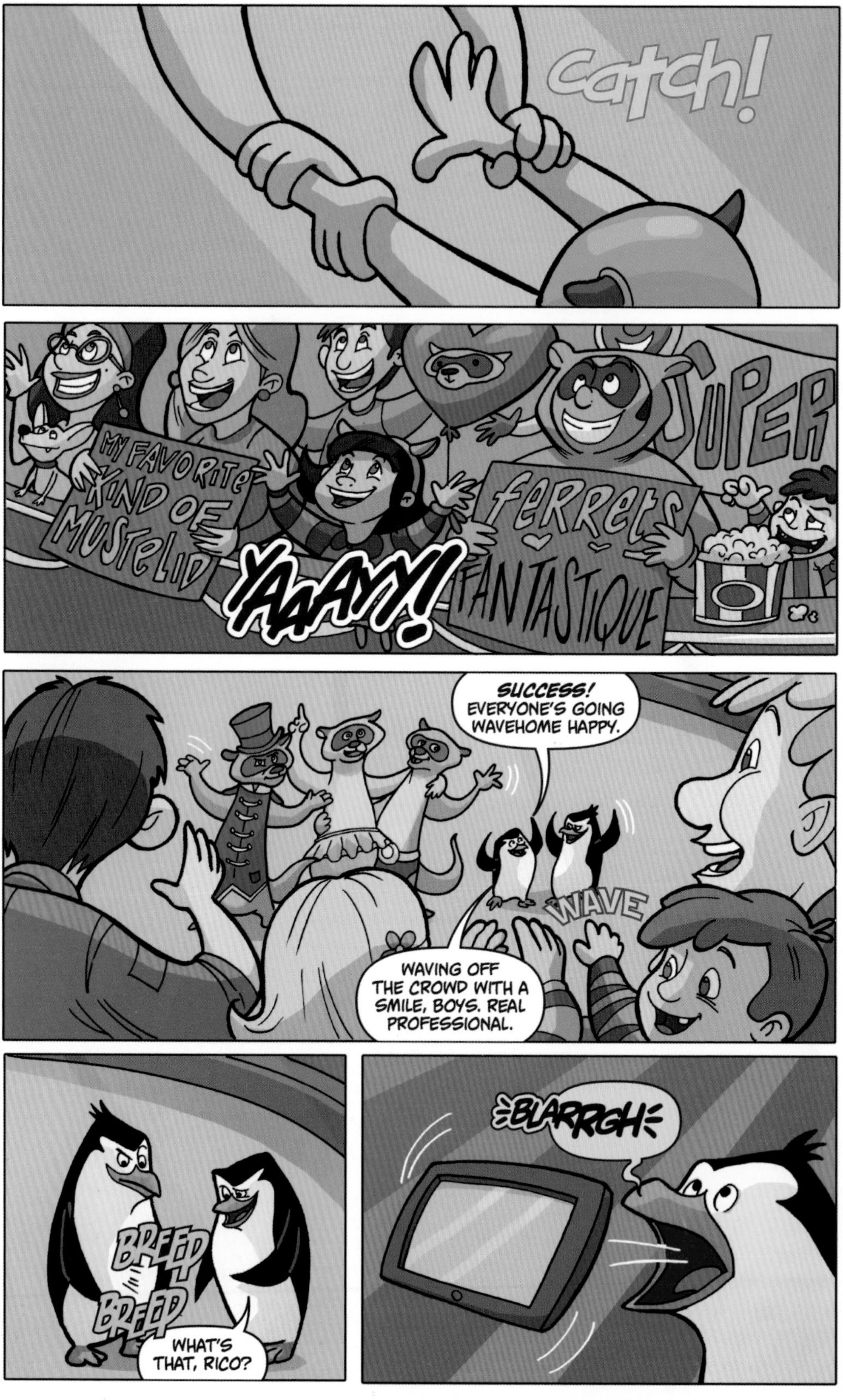
CATCH!
MY FAVORITE KIND OF MUSTELID
YAAAYY!
FERRETS ♡ FANTASTIQUE
SUPER
SUCCESS! EVERYONE'S GOING WAVEHOME HAPPY.
WAVE
WAVING OFF THE CROWD WITH A SMILE, BOYS. REAL PROFESSIONAL.
BREEP
BREEP
WHAT'S THAT, RICO?
BLARRGH

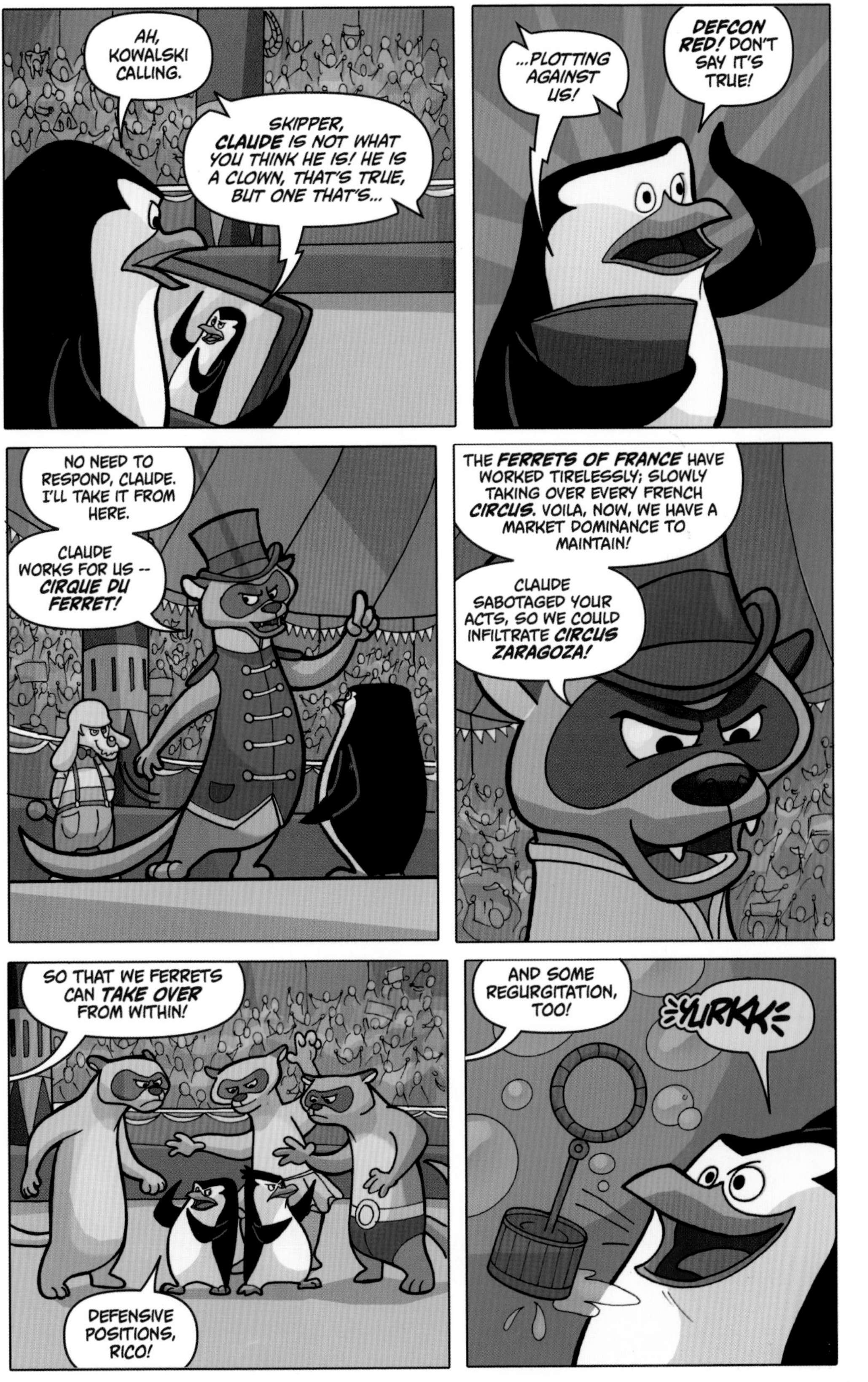
AH, KOWALSKI CALLING.
SKIPPER, CLAUDE IS NOT WHAT YOU THINK HE IS! HE IS A CLOWN, THAT'S TRUE, BUT ONE THAT'S...
...PLOTTING AGAINST US!
DEFCON RED! DON'T SAY IT'S TRUE!
NO NEED TO RESPOND, CLAUDE. I'LL TAKE IT FROM HERE.
CLAUDE WORKS FOR US -- CIRQUE DU FERRET!
THE FERRETS OF FRANCE HAVE WORKED TIRELESSLY; SLOWLY TAKING OVER EVERY FRENCH CIRCUS. VOILA, NOW, WE HAVE A MARKET DOMINANCE TO MAINTAIN!
CLAUDE SABOTAGED YOUR ACTS, SO WE COULD INFILTRATE CIRCUS ZARAGOZA!
SO THAT WE FERRETS CAN TAKE OVER FROM WITHIN!
DEFENSIVE POSITIONS, RICO!
AND SOME REGURGITATION, TOO!
YURKK

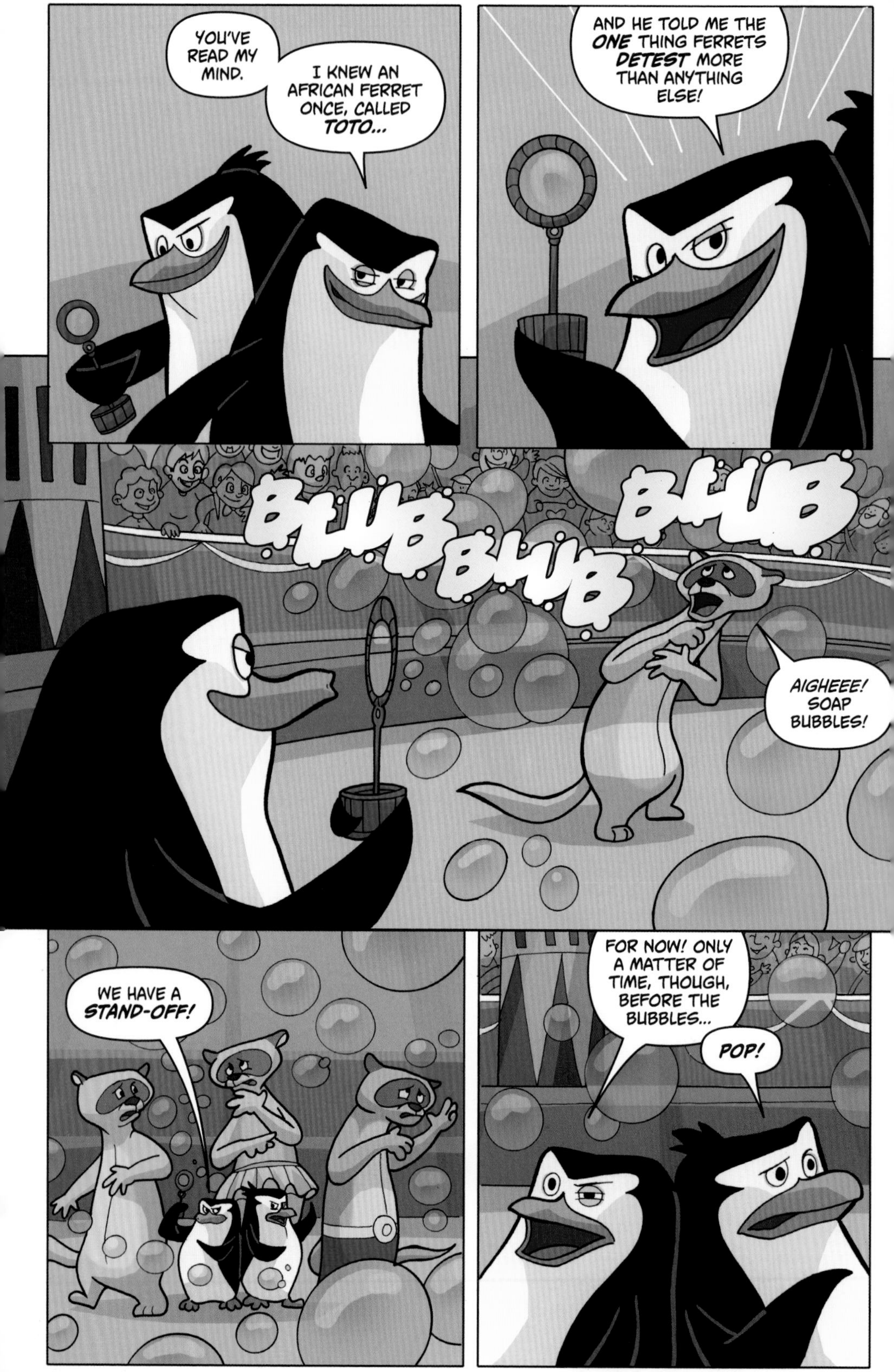
YOU'VE READ MY MIND.
I KNEW AN AFRICAN FERRET ONCE, CALLED TOTO...
AND HE TOLD ME THE ONE THING FERRETS DETEST MORE THAN ANYTHING ELSE!
BLUB BLUB BLUB
AIGHEEE! SOAP BUBBLES!
WE HAVE A STAND-OFF!
FOR NOW! ONLY A MATTER OF TIME, THOUGH, BEFORE THE BUBBLES...
POP!

MEANWHILE, OFF-STAGE...

AND WHERE, MISTER CLOWN, DO YOU THINK YOU ARE CREEPING OFF TO?

WHAT?! OH, IT'S THE SCAREDY-CAT PENGUIN.

WAIT A MINUTE! YOUR NOSE...!

THAT'S ONE OF MINE!

grab

GIVE IT BACK!

PLENTY MORE WHERE THAT CAME FROM.

YOU SEE, I'M NO LONGER SCARED OF YOU. I'VE CONQUERED MY FEAR OF CLOWNS!

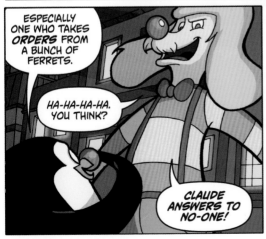

ESPECIALLY ONE WHO TAKES *ORDERS* FROM A BUNCH OF FERRETS.

HA-HA-HA-HA. YOU THINK?

CLAUDE ANSWERS TO NO-ONE!

WHAT WE HAVE IS *PENGUIN V FERRET* IN THE BATTLE FOR THE BIG TOP. THIS IS ALL PART OF THE PLAN -- *CLAUDE'S PLAN!*

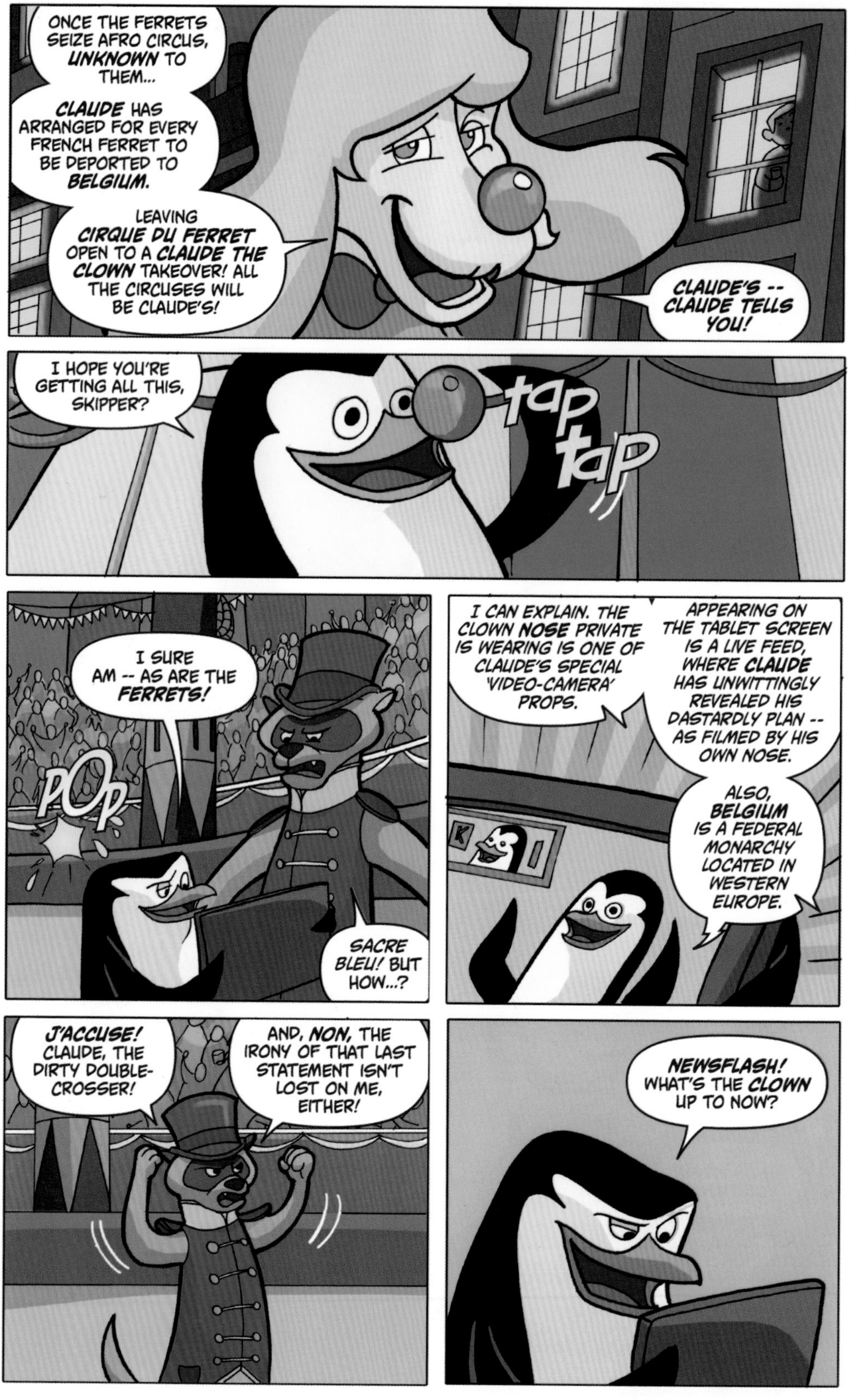
ONCE THE FERRETS SEIZE AFRO CIRCUS, UNKNOWN TO THEM...
CLAUDE HAS ARRANGED FOR EVERY FRENCH FERRET TO BE DEPORTED TO BELGIUM.
LEAVING CIRQUE DU FERRET OPEN TO A CLAUDE THE CLOWN TAKEOVER! ALL THE CIRCUSES WILL BE CLAUDE'S!
CLAUDE'S -- CLAUDE TELLS YOU!
I HOPE YOU'RE GETTING ALL THIS, SKIPPER?
tap tap
I SURE AM -- AS ARE THE FERRETS!
POP
SACRE BLEU! BUT HOW...?
I CAN EXPLAIN. THE CLOWN NOSE PRIVATE IS WEARING IS ONE OF CLAUDE'S SPECIAL 'VIDEO-CAMERA' PROPS.
APPEARING ON THE TABLET SCREEN IS A LIVE FEED, WHERE CLAUDE HAS UNWITTINGLY REVEALED HIS DASTARDLY PLAN -- AS FILMED BY HIS OWN NOSE.
ALSO, BELGIUM IS A FEDERAL MONARCHY LOCATED IN WESTERN EUROPE.
J'ACCUSE! CLAUDE, THE DIRTY DOUBLE-CROSSER!
AND, NON, THE IRONY OF THAT LAST STATEMENT ISN'T LOST ON ME, EITHER!
NEWSFLASH! WHAT'S THE CLOWN UP TO NOW?

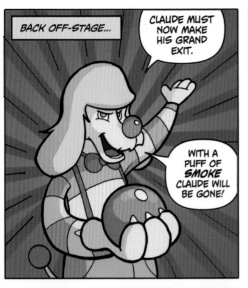

BACK OFF-STAGE...

CLAUDE MUST NOW MAKE HIS GRAND EXIT.

WITH A PUFF OF *SMOKE* CLAUDE WILL BE GONE!

EH? OH, OKAY, CHEERIO, THEN!

BOOM

THE *NOSE* CLAUDE GRABBED FROM YOU...?

NOT A *'SMOKE PELLET'* NOSE, BUT ⸨CROAK⸩ AN *'EXPLODING'* NOSE...?

UMM... OUI.

NOW THAT CLAUDE IS OUT FOR THE COUNT, WE'LL CONTACT THE RELEVANT AUTHORITIES AND SEND HIM TO CLOWN PRISON.

CLOWN PRISON? THERE IS NO SUCH THING AS -- *OH*, NEVER MIND.

≥GULP≤

PENGUIN AGAINST FERRET IN THE BATTLE OF THE *BIG TOP*, I'D CALL IT A SCORE DRAW.

WE CAN BOTH PUT THIS CLAUDE BUSINESS BEHIND US, MONSIEUR FERRET, SO WHAT DO YOU SAY -- PARTNERS?

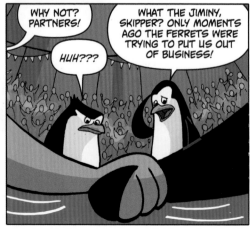

WHY NOT? PARTNERS!

HUH???

WHAT THE JIMINY, SKIPPER? ONLY MOMENTS AGO THE FERRETS WERE TRYING TO PUT US OUT OF BUSINESS!

≥PSST≤

AGREED, BUT IT'S EITHER THIS OR KEEP THEM AS *PETS*!

THE END!

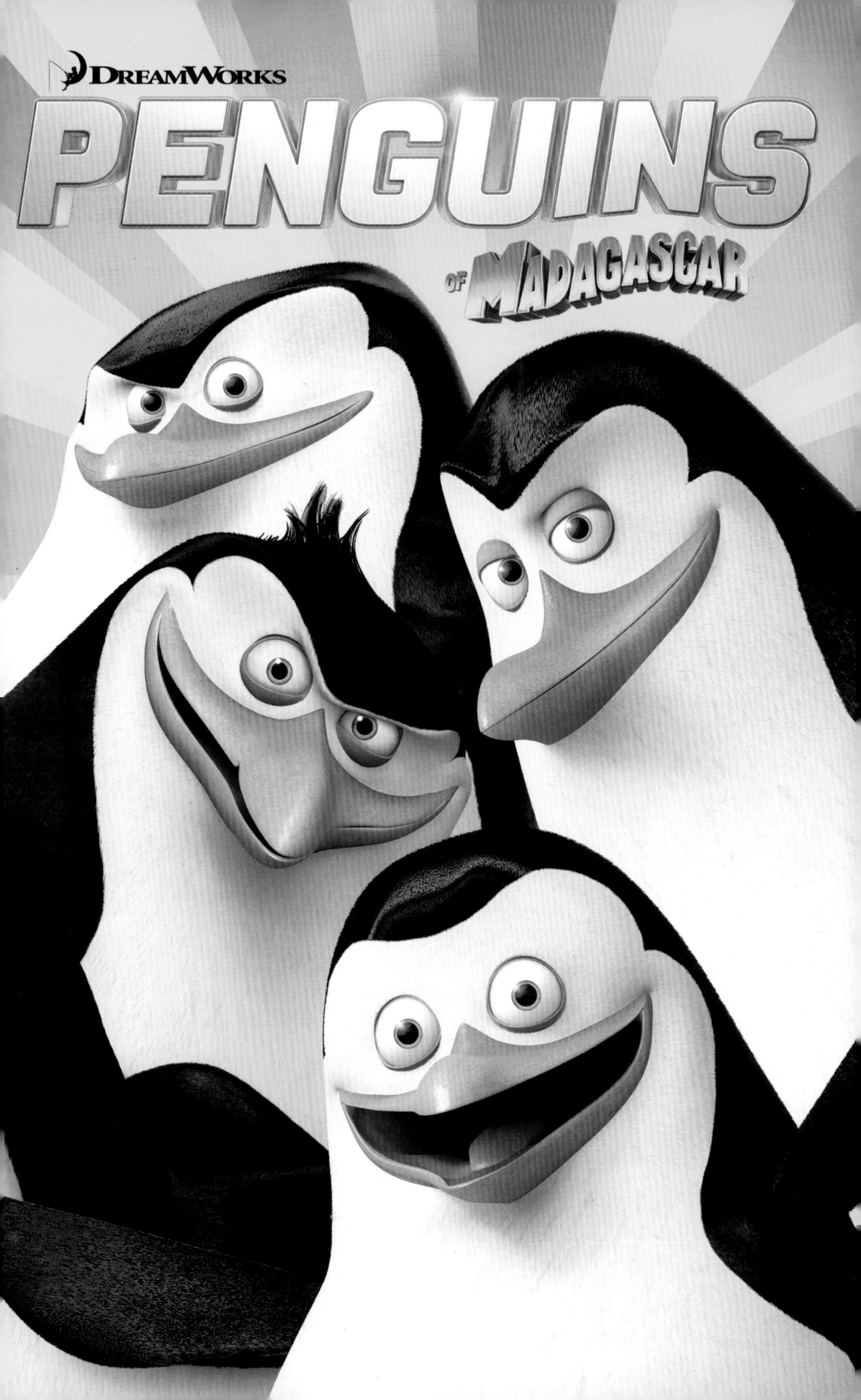
DreamWorks
PENGUINS
OF MADAGASCAR

How To...

Skipper's Guide t Being a

If you want to be a commando, you're going to have to learn the basics. So if you really think you've got what it takes, read these top tips to being the best!

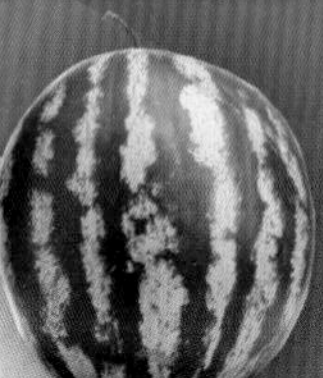

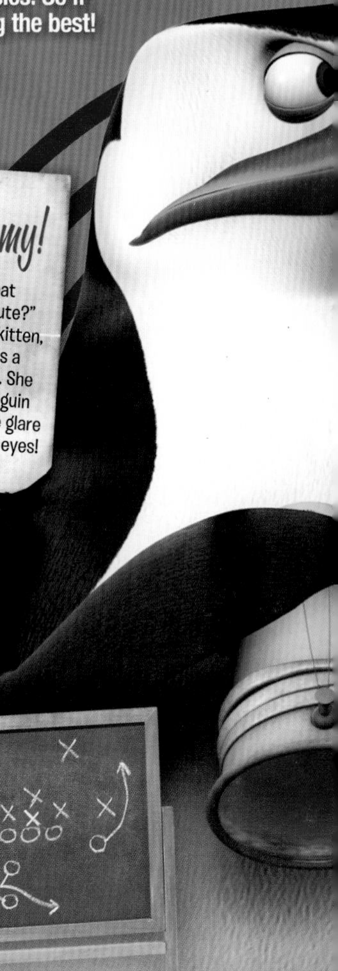

On guard!

A trip to the shops is never just a trip to the shops. Could the cheese slices be booby-trapped? Why is that melon looking at me funny? These are the things you MUST ask yourself on every mission!

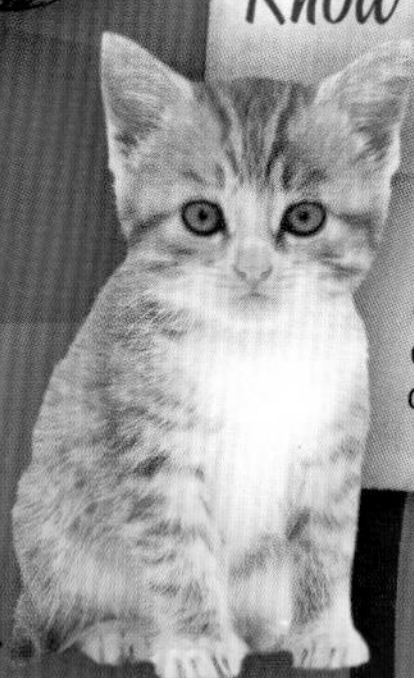

Know your enemy!

"Aww look at that kitten! Isn't it cute?" NO NO NO! That kitten, most probably, is a trained assassin. She could take a penguin out with just one glare of her evil kitten eyes!

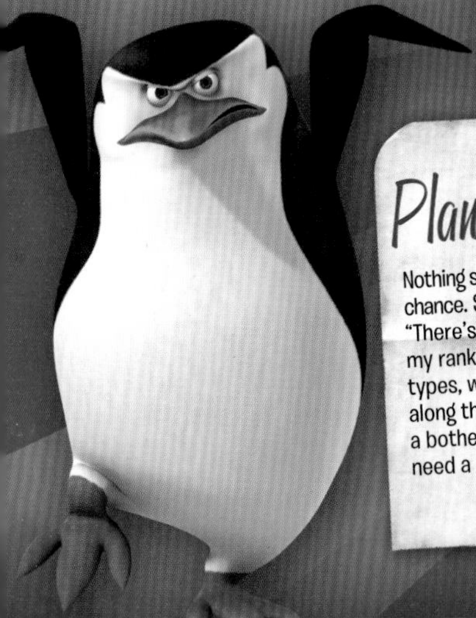

Plan, plan, plan!

Nothing should be left to chance. Skipper's motto is: "There's no place among my ranks for carefree types, who like to drift along through life with not a bother in the world." You need a plan A, B, C and Z!

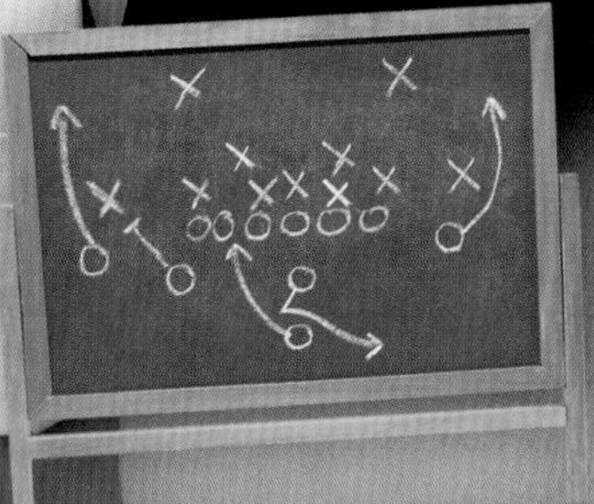

Commando Test

Can you crack this code using the key underneath?

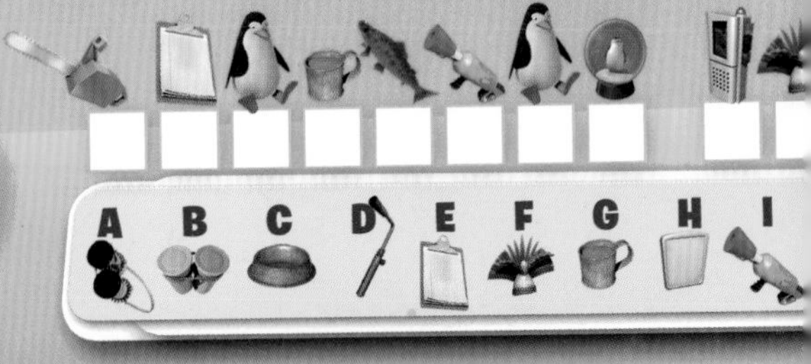
A
B
C
D
E
F
G
H
I

COMMANDO!

Get to the point!

If you have a clear goal, stick to it. Don't listen to other people (like Kowalski) trying to meddle and interfere with their pesky organization and planning...

To be forewarned is to be forearmed!

Information is key. Find out as much as possible before every mission. Who is going to be there? What day is it? Who are you? Who am I? Do you have a spare kipper in your pocket? These sorts of questions are essential.

Code words

The best code words are those that have nothing to do with what you're trying to say. It's best to tell your colleagues about the code words, however, or you could get yourself in big trouble. Rico once confused the code word "lion" and it wasn't pretty!

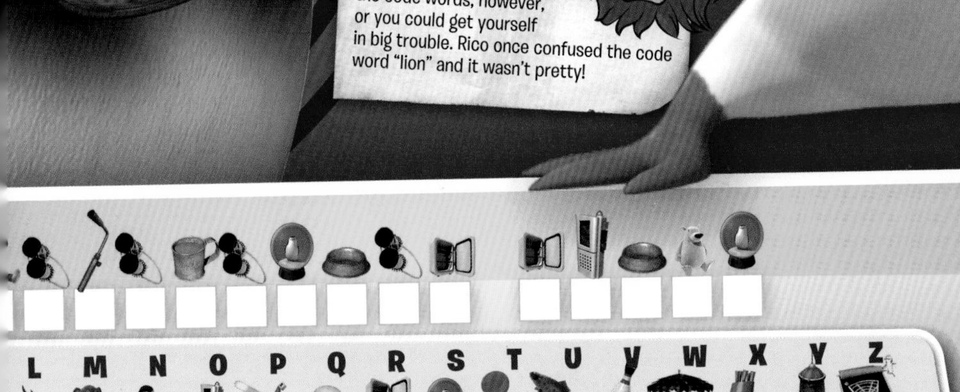

Answer: Penguins of Madagascar rocks!

L M N O P Q R S T U V W X Y Z

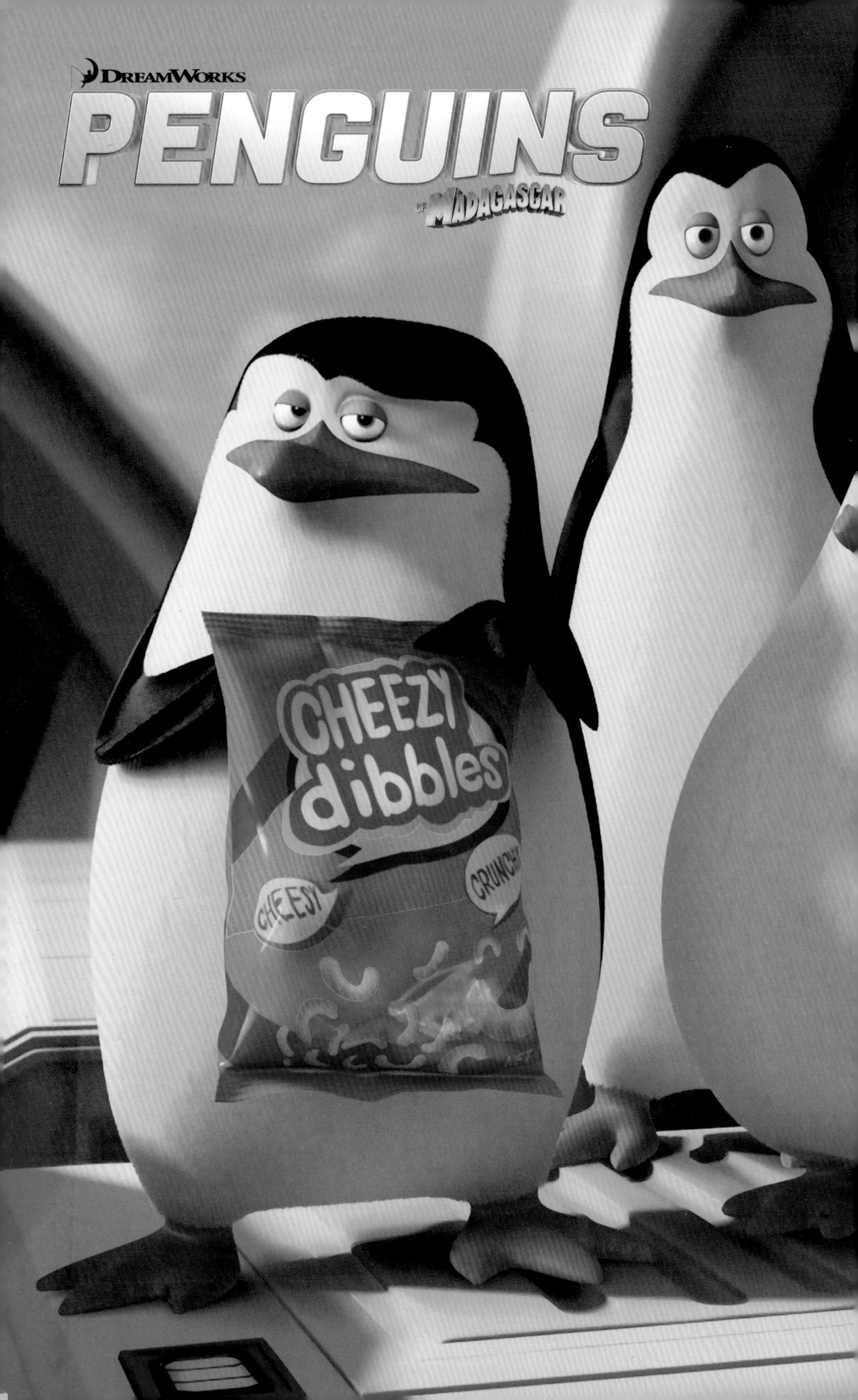
DreamWorks
PENGUINS
of MADAGASCAR
CHEEZY dibbles
CHEESY

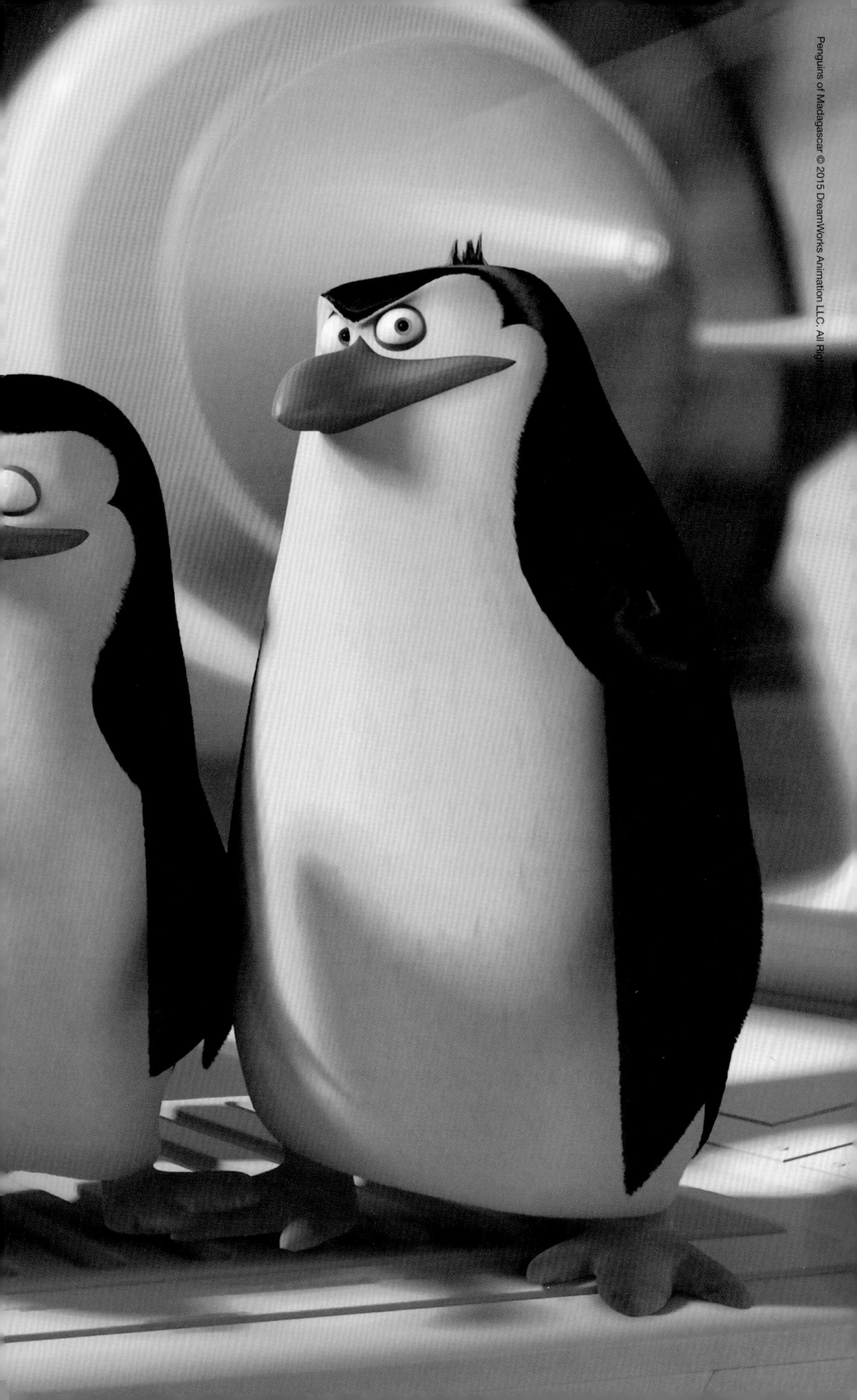

OPERATION: HEIST

SCRIPT
Cavan Scott

ART
Lucas Ferreyra

LETTERING
Jim Campbell

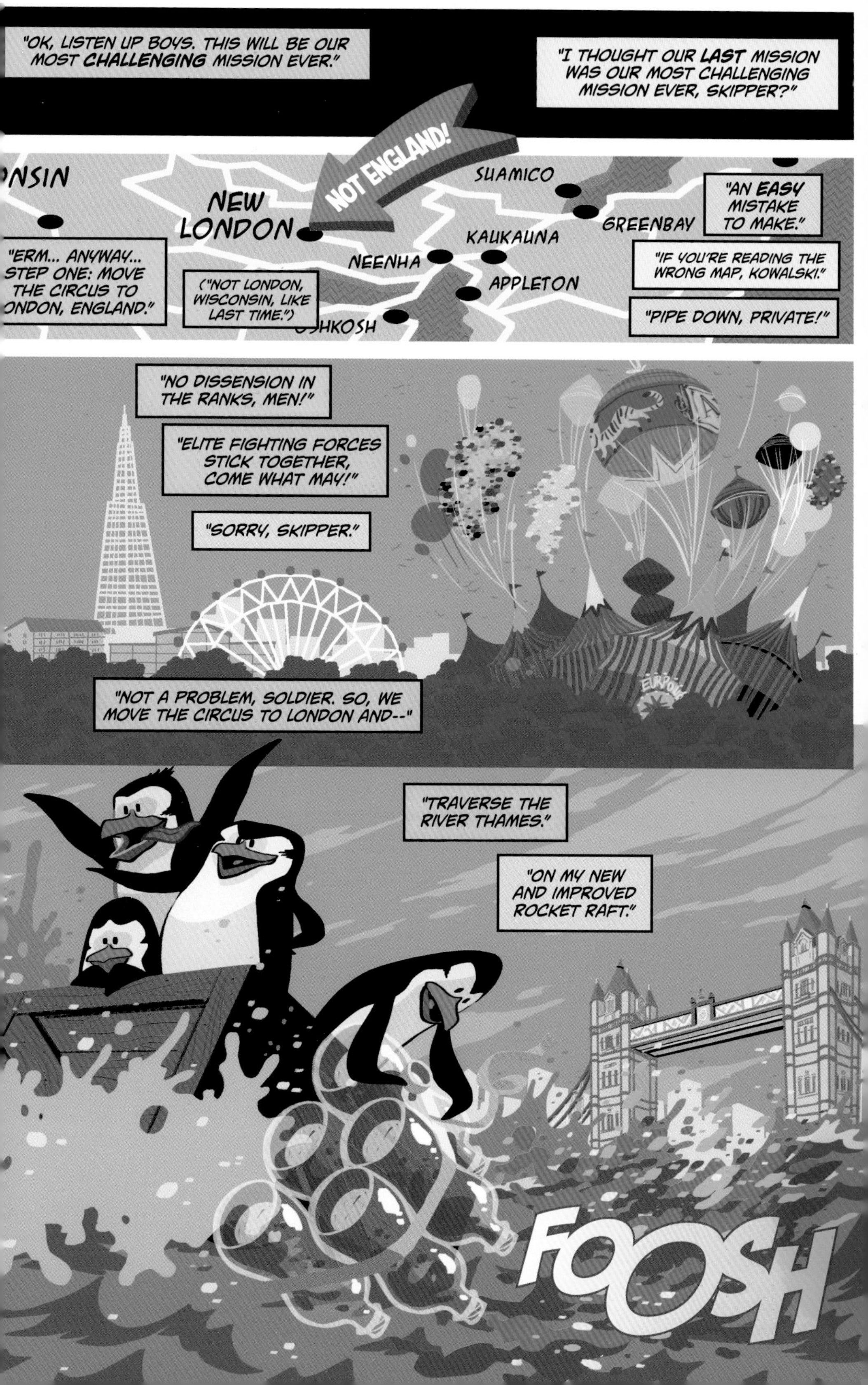
"OK, LISTEN UP BOYS. THIS WILL BE OUR MOST CHALLENGING MISSION EVER."
"I THOUGHT OUR LAST MISSION WAS OUR MOST CHALLENGING MISSION EVER, SKIPPER?"
NOT ENGLAND!
NSIN
NEW LONDON
SUAMICO
GREENBAY
KAUKAUNA
NEENHA
APPLETON
OSHKOSH
"ERM... ANYWAY... STEP ONE: MOVE THE CIRCUS TO LONDON, ENGLAND."
("NOT LONDON, WISCONSIN, LIKE LAST TIME.")
"AN EASY MISTAKE TO MAKE."
"IF YOU'RE READING THE WRONG MAP, KOWALSKI."
"PIPE DOWN, PRIVATE!"
"NO DISSENSION IN THE RANKS, MEN!"
"ELITE FIGHTING FORCES STICK TOGETHER, COME WHAT MAY!"
"SORRY, SKIPPER."
"NOT A PROBLEM, SOLDIER. SO, WE MOVE THE CIRCUS TO LONDON AND--"
"TRAVERSE THE RIVER THAMES."
"ON MY NEW AND IMPROVED ROCKET RAFT."
FOOSH

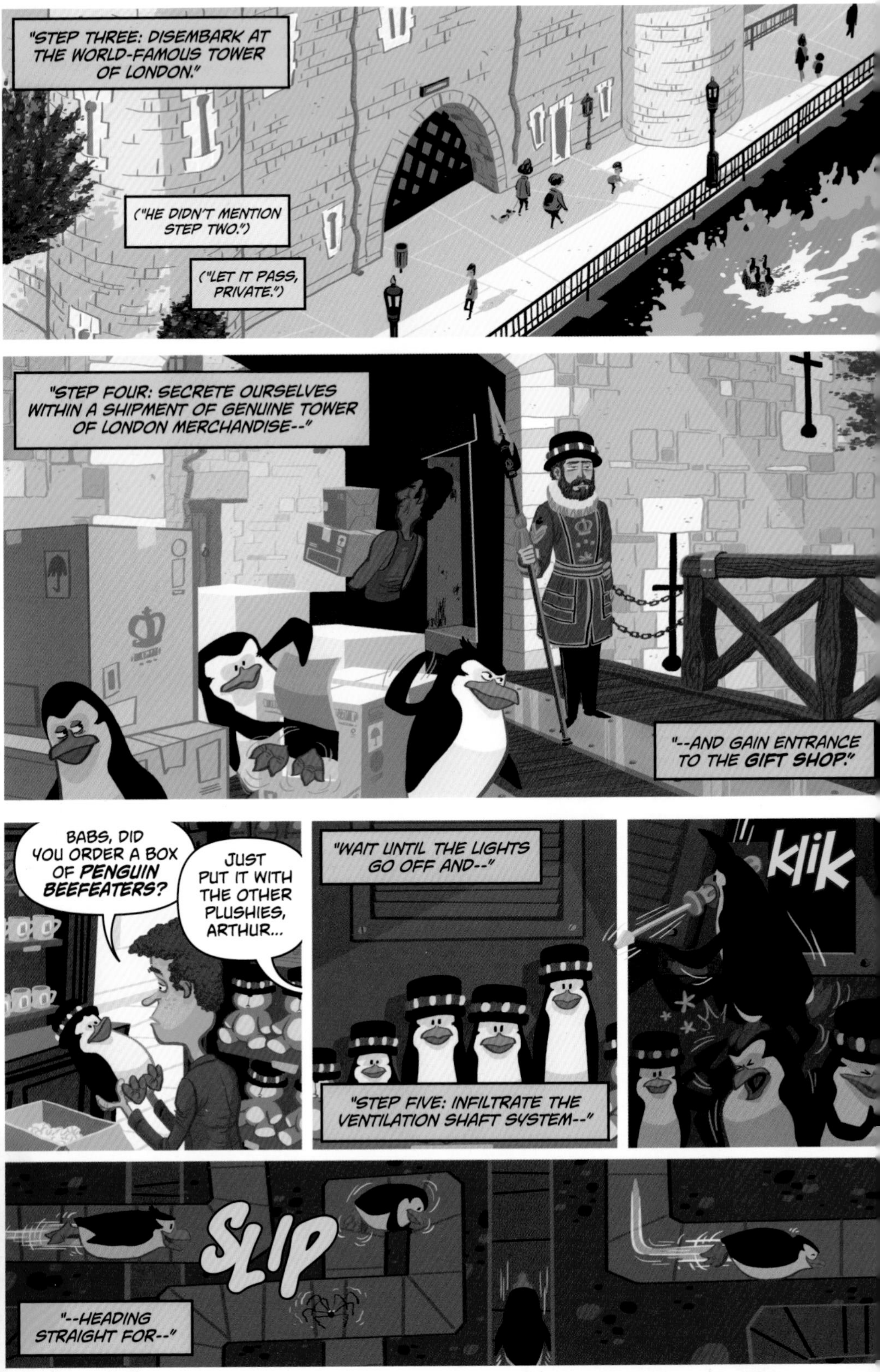
"STEP THREE: DISEMBARK AT THE WORLD-FAMOUS TOWER OF LONDON."
("HE DIDN'T MENTION STEP TWO.")
("LET IT PASS, PRIVATE.")
"STEP FOUR: SECRETE OURSELVES WITHIN A SHIPMENT OF GENUINE TOWER OF LONDON MERCHANDISE--"
"--AND GAIN ENTRANCE TO THE GIFT SHOP."
BABS, DID YOU ORDER A BOX OF PENGUIN BEEFEATERS?
JUST PUT IT WITH THE OTHER PLUSHIES, ARTHUR...
"WAIT UNTIL THE LIGHTS GO OFF AND--"
"STEP FIVE: INFILTRATE THE VENTILATION SHAFT SYSTEM--"
KLIK
SLIP
"--HEADING STRAIGHT FOR--"

"--THE CROWN JEWELS!"
SKIPPER, DO YOU THINK THIS IS SUCH A GOOD IDEA?
BREAKING INTO THE MOST SECURE FORTRESS IN ENGLAND TO STEAL THE CROWN JEWELS DURING THE MIDDLE OF A CRIMEWAVE THAT IS ROCKING LONDON TO ITS KNEES?
OPERATION: HEIST

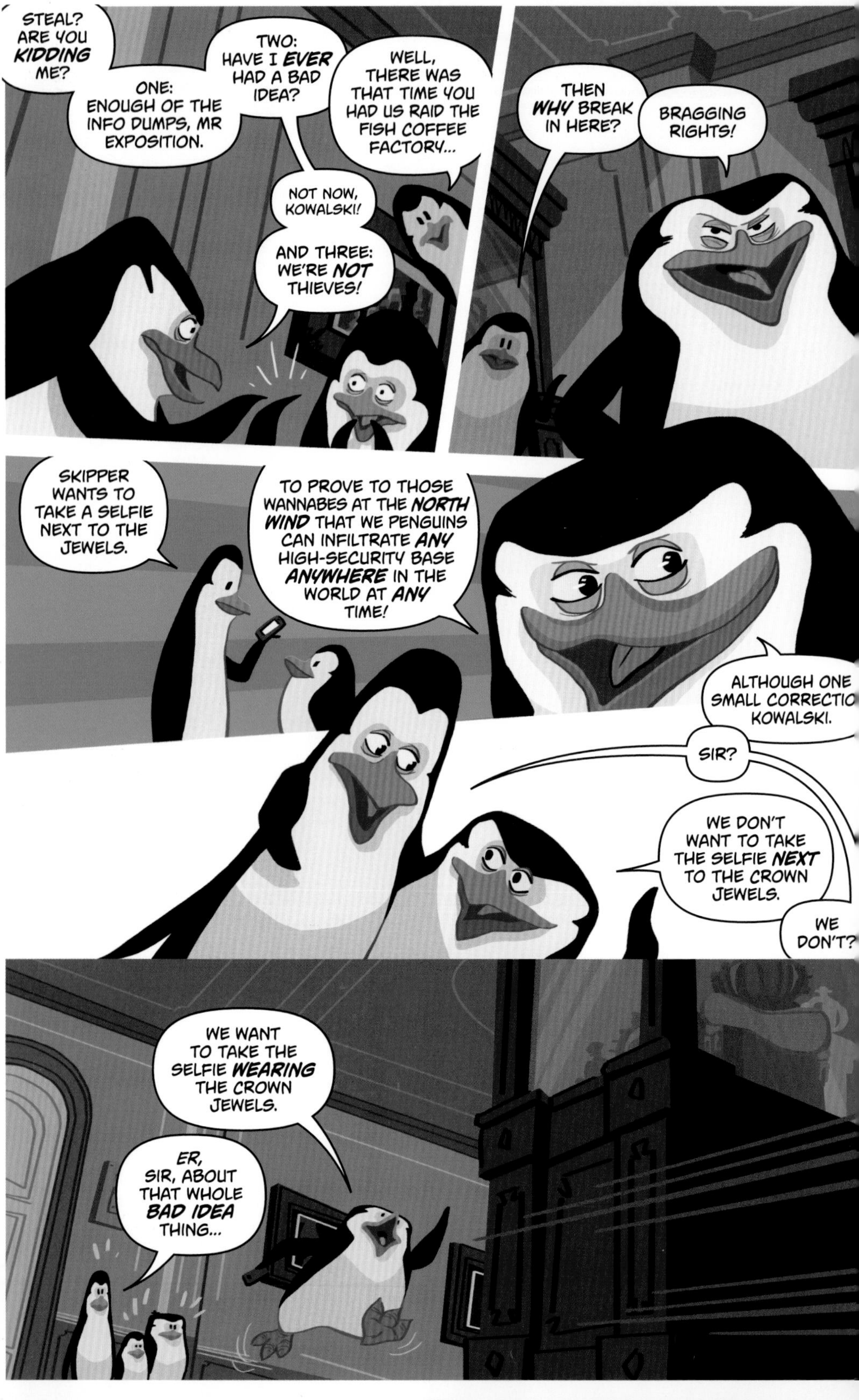
STEAL? ARE YOU *KIDDING* ME?
ONE: ENOUGH OF THE INFO DUMPS, MR EXPOSITION.
TWO: HAVE I *EVER* HAD A BAD IDEA?
WELL, THERE WAS THAT TIME YOU HAD US RAID THE FISH COFFEE FACTORY...
NOT NOW, KOWALSKI!
AND THREE: WE'RE *NOT* THIEVES!
THEN *WHY* BREAK IN HERE?
BRAGGING RIGHTS!
SKIPPER WANTS TO TAKE A SELFIE NEXT TO THE JEWELS.
TO PROVE TO THOSE WANNABES AT THE *NORTH WIND* THAT WE PENGUINS CAN INFILTRATE *ANY* HIGH-SECURITY BASE *ANYWHERE* IN THE WORLD AT *ANY* TIME!
ALTHOUGH ONE SMALL CORRECTIO KOWALSKI.
SIR?
WE DON'T WANT TO TAKE THE SELFIE *NEXT* TO THE CROWN JEWELS.
WE DON'T?
WE WANT TO TAKE THE SELFIE *WEARING* THE CROWN JEWELS.
ER, SIR, ABOUT THAT WHOLE *BAD IDEA* THING...

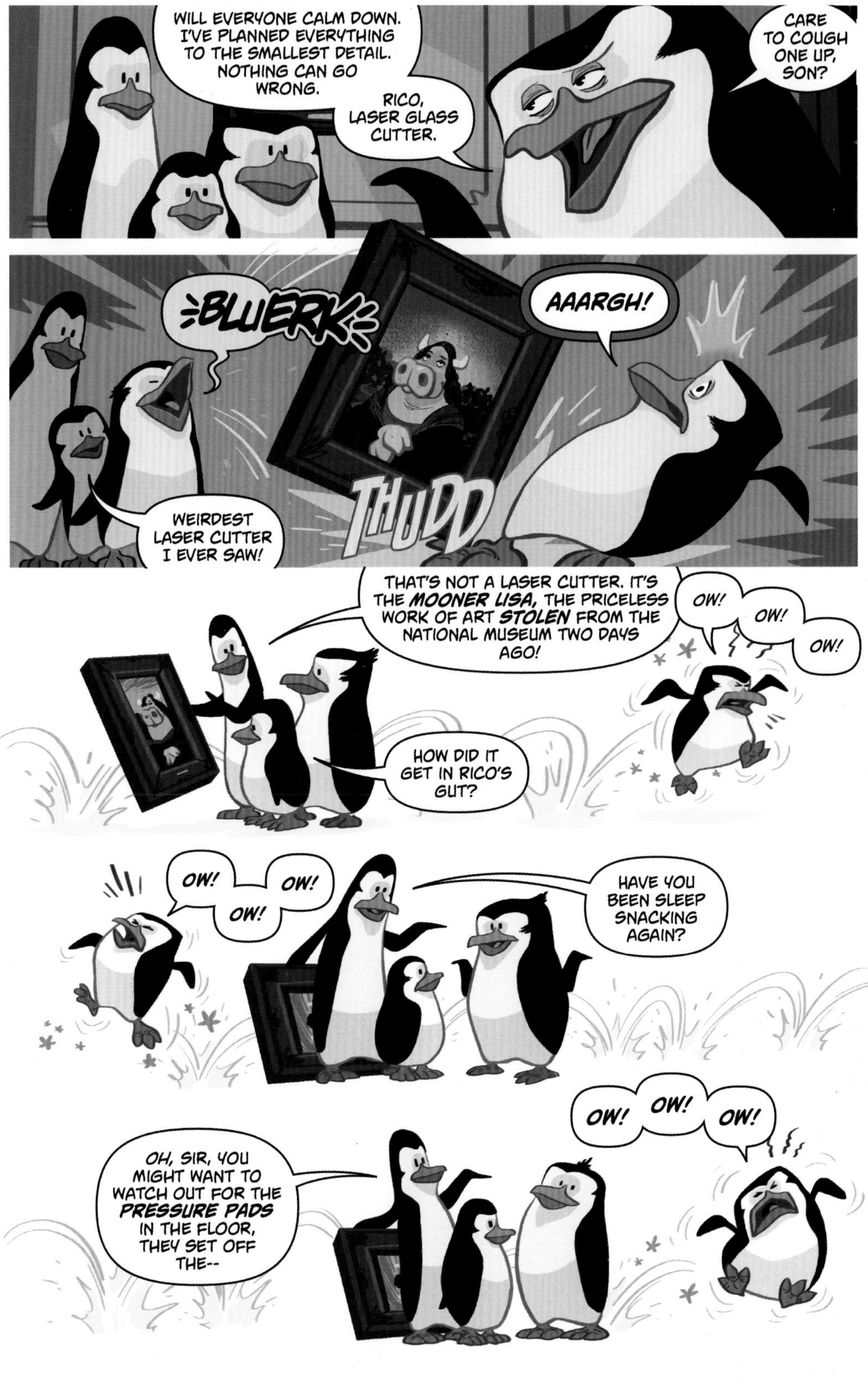
WILL EVERYONE CALM DOWN. I'VE PLANNED EVERYTHING TO THE SMALLEST DETAIL. NOTHING CAN GO WRONG.
RICO, LASER GLASS CUTTER.
CARE TO COUGH ONE UP, SON?
BLUERK
AAARGH!
THUDD
WEIRDEST LASER CUTTER I EVER SAW!
THAT'S NOT A LASER CUTTER. IT'S THE MOONER LISA, THE PRICELESS WORK OF ART STOLEN FROM THE NATIONAL MUSEUM TWO DAYS AGO!
OW!
OW!
OW!
HOW DID IT GET IN RICO'S GUT?
OW!
OW!
OW!
HAVE YOU BEEN SLEEP SNACKING AGAIN?
OW!
OW!
OW!
OH, SIR, YOU MIGHT WANT TO WATCH OUT FOR THE PRESSURE PADS IN THE FLOOR, THEY SET OFF THE--

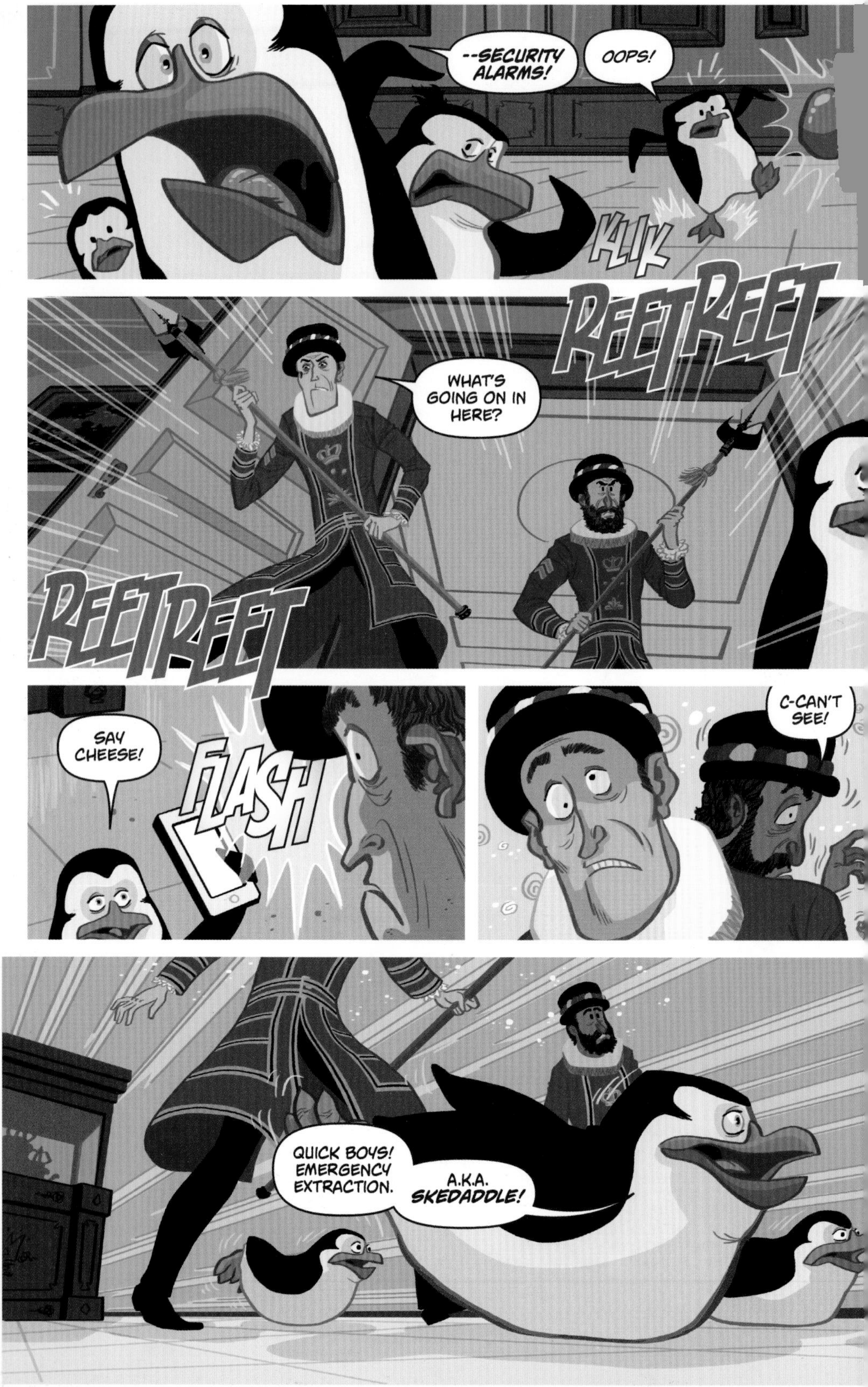
--SECURITY ALARMS!
OOPS!
KLIK
REETREET
WHAT'S GOING ON IN HERE?
REETREET
SAY CHEESE!
FLASH
C-CAN'T SEE!
QUICK BOYS! EMERGENCY EXTRACTION.
A.K.A. SKEDADDLE!

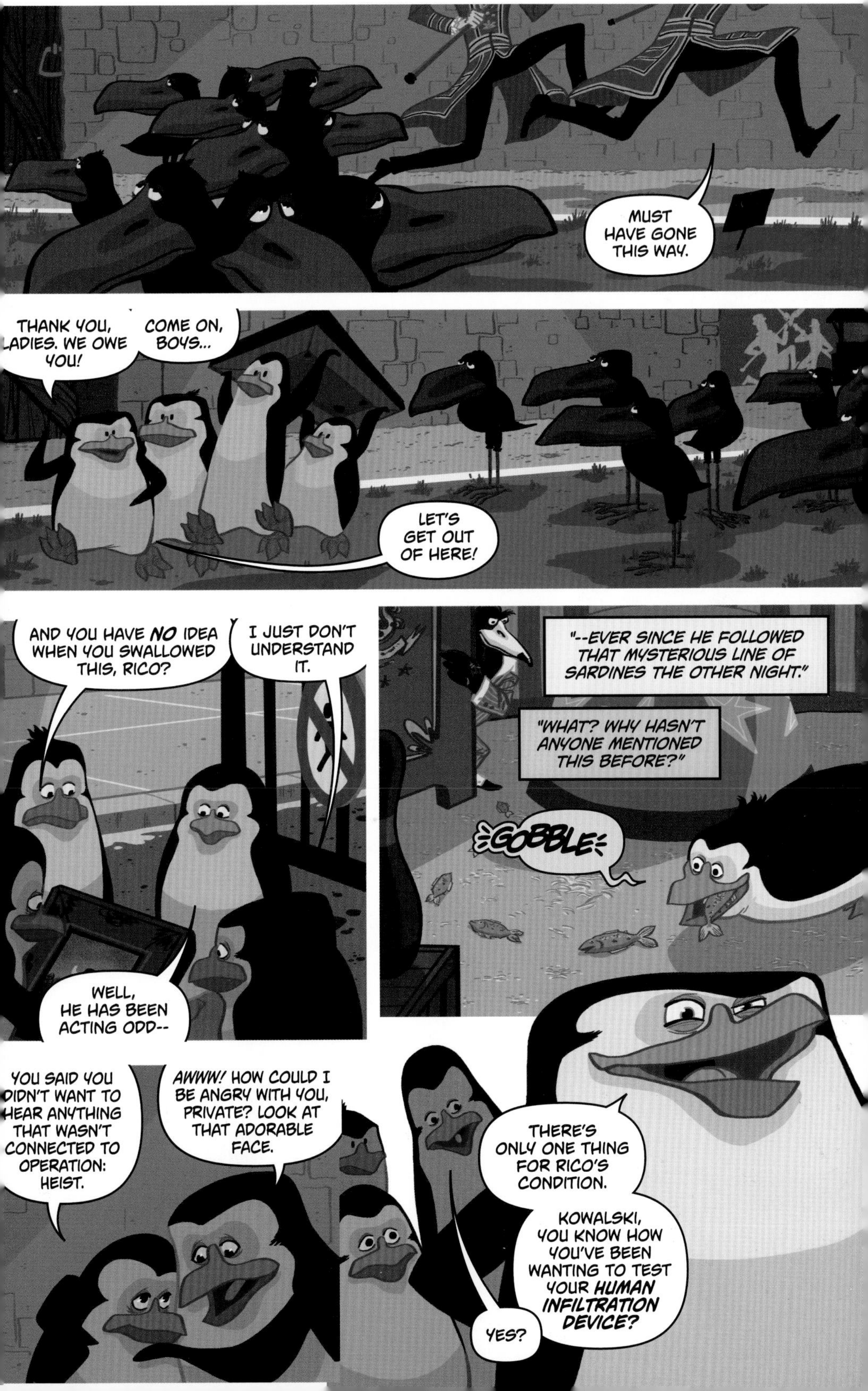
MUST HAVE GONE THIS WAY.
THANK YOU, LADIES. WE OWE YOU!
COME ON, BOYS...
LET'S GET OUT OF HERE!
AND YOU HAVE NO IDEA WHEN YOU SWALLOWED THIS, RICO?
I JUST DON'T UNDERSTAND IT.
WELL, HE HAS BEEN ACTING ODD--
"--EVER SINCE HE FOLLOWED THAT MYSTERIOUS LINE OF SARDINES THE OTHER NIGHT."
"WHAT? WHY HASN'T ANYONE MENTIONED THIS BEFORE?"
GOBBLE
YOU SAID YOU DIDN'T WANT TO HEAR ANYTHING THAT WASN'T CONNECTED TO OPERATION: HEIST.
AWWW! HOW COULD I BE ANGRY WITH YOU, PRIVATE? LOOK AT THAT ADORABLE FACE.
THERE'S ONLY ONE THING FOR RICO'S CONDITION.
KOWALSKI, YOU KNOW HOW YOU'VE BEEN WANTING TO TEST YOUR HUMAN INFILTRATION DEVICE?
YES?

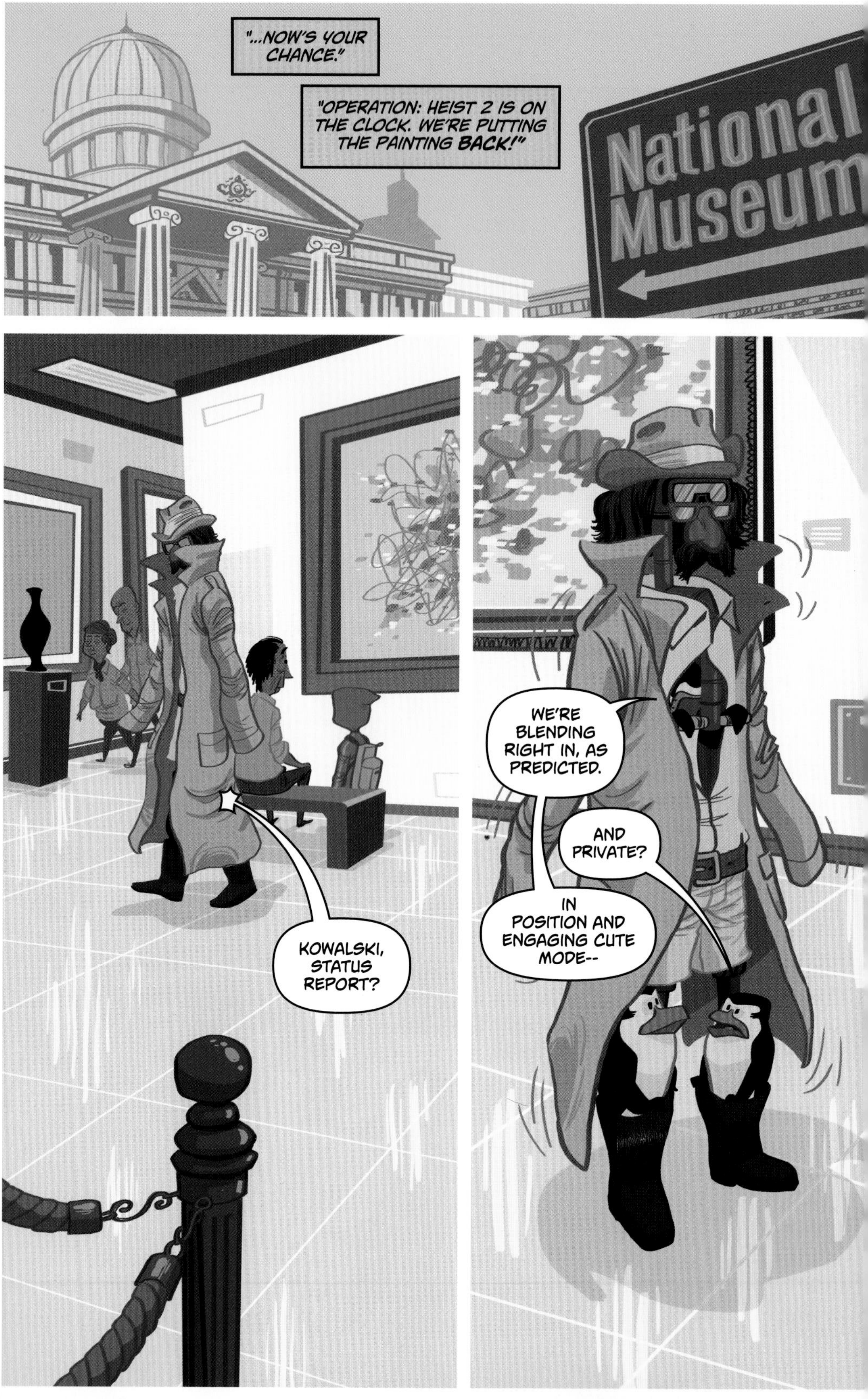
"...NOW'S YOUR CHANCE."
"OPERATION: HEIST 2 IS ON THE CLOCK. WE'RE PUTTING THE PAINTING **BACK!**"
National Museum
KOWALSKI, STATUS REPORT?
WE'RE BLENDING RIGHT IN, AS PREDICTED.
AND PRIVATE?
IN POSITION AND ENGAGING CUTE MODE--

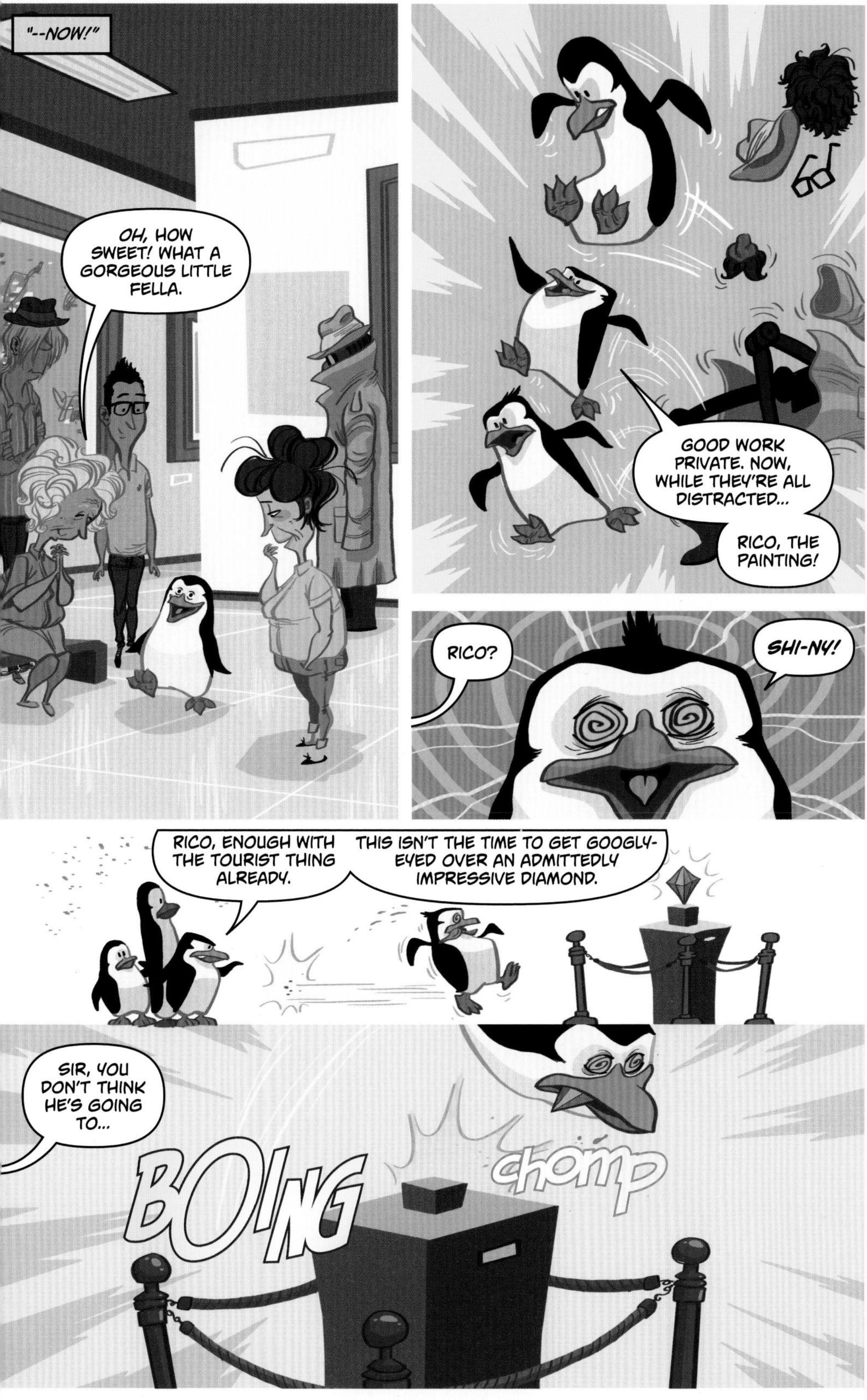
"--NOW!"
OH, HOW SWEET! WHAT A GORGEOUS LITTLE FELLA.
GOOD WORK PRIVATE. NOW, WHILE THEY'RE ALL DISTRACTED...
RICO, THE PAINTING!
RICO?
SHI-NY!
RICO, ENOUGH WITH THE TOURIST THING ALREADY.
THIS ISN'T THE TIME TO GET GOOGLY-EYED OVER AN ADMITTEDLY IMPRESSIVE DIAMOND.
SIR, YOU DON'T THINK HE'S GOING TO...
BOING
chomp

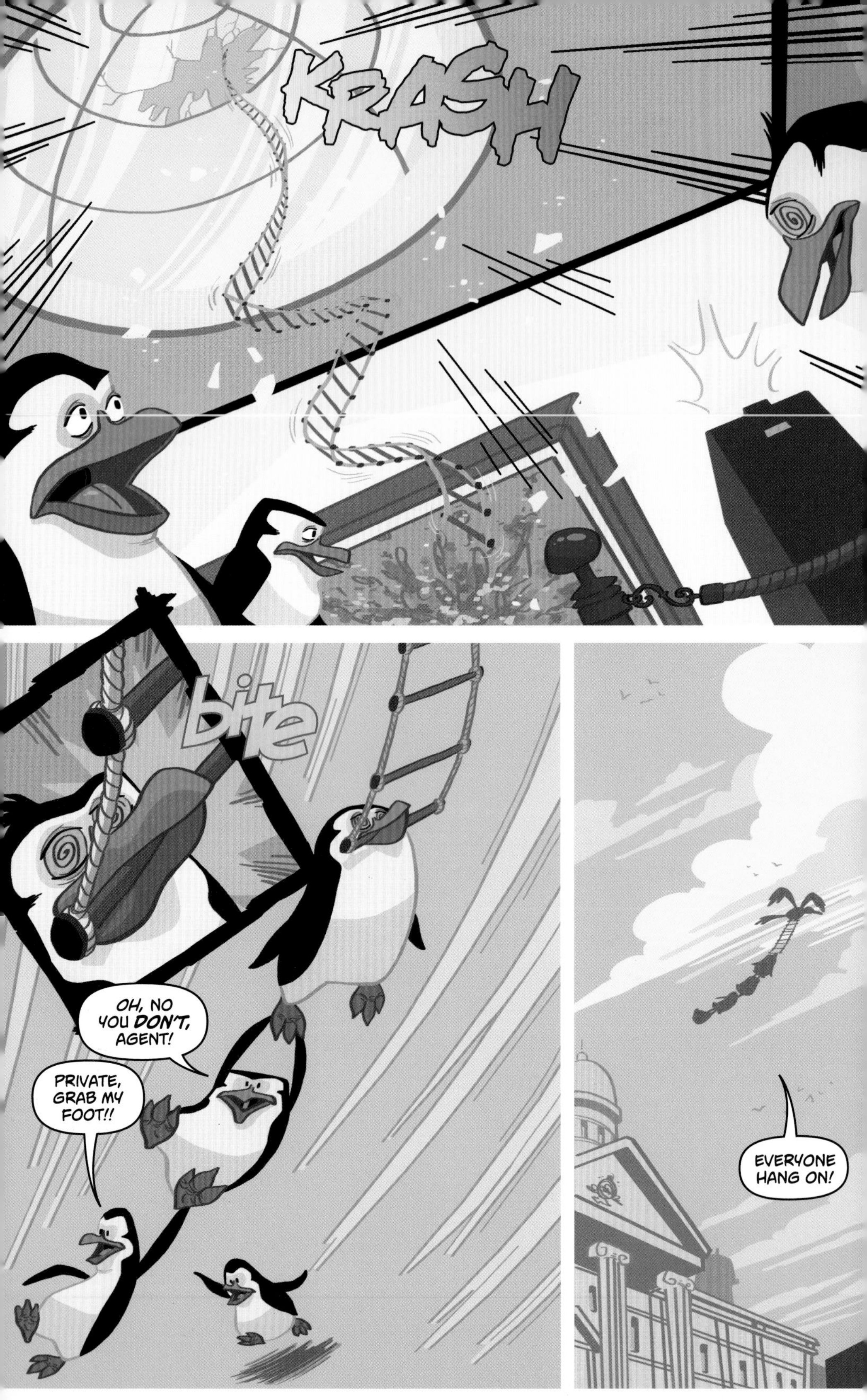
KRASH
bite
OH, NO YOU DON'T, AGENT!
PRIVATE, GRAB MY FOOT!!
EVERYONE HANG ON!

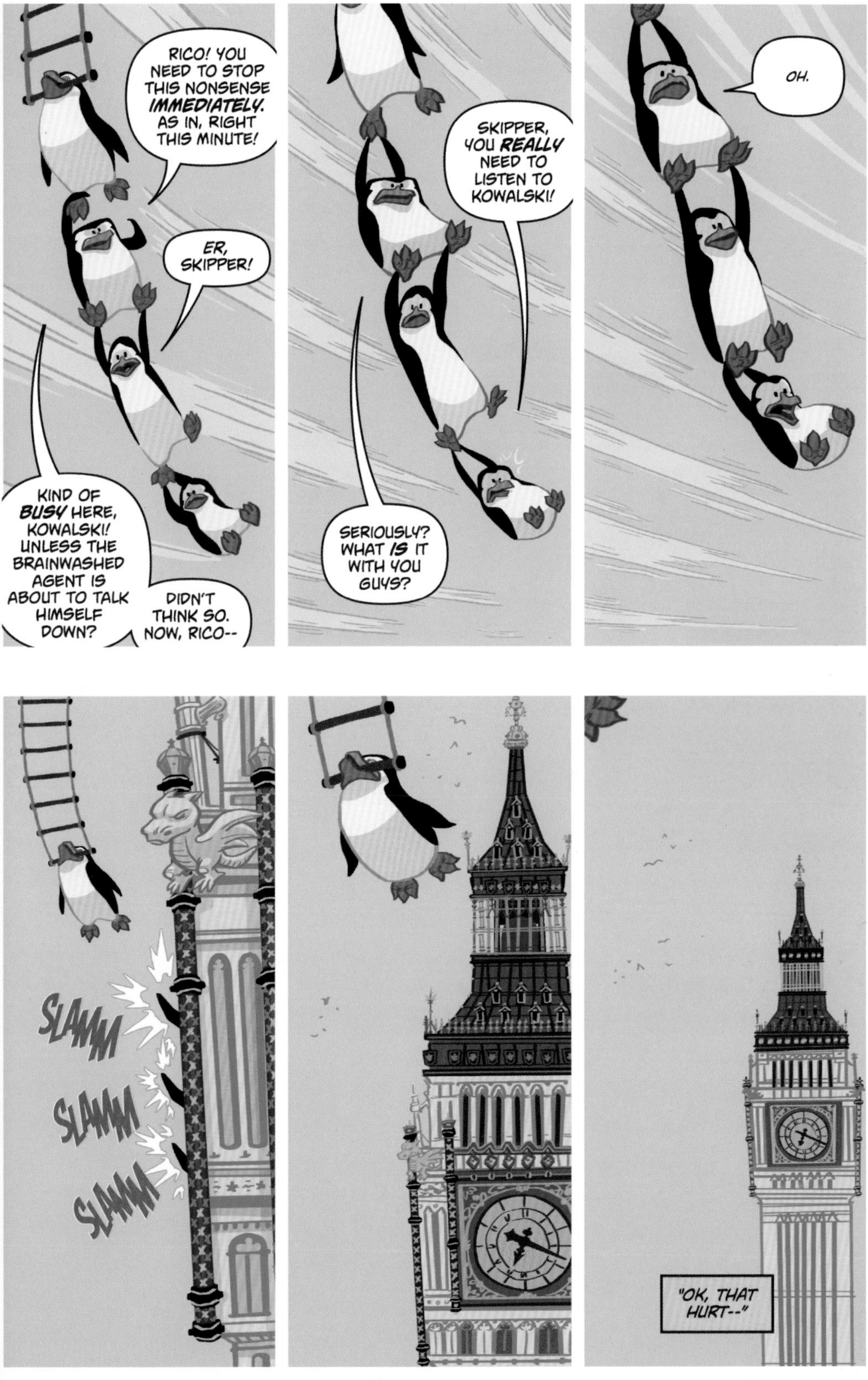
RICO! YOU NEED TO STOP THIS NONSENSE IMMEDIATELY. AS IN, RIGHT THIS MINUTE!
ER, SKIPPER!
KIND OF BUSY HERE, KOWALSKI! UNLESS THE BRAINWASHED AGENT IS ABOUT TO TALK HIMSELF DOWN?
DIDN'T THINK SO. NOW, RICO--
SKIPPER, YOU REALLY NEED TO LISTEN TO KOWALSKI!
SERIOUSLY? WHAT IS IT WITH YOU GUYS?
OH.
SLAMM
SLAMM
SLAMM
"OK, THAT HURT--"

"--BUT WE HAVE A ROGUE AGENT...

AND WE NEED TO BRING HIM HOME.

KOWALSKI? INTELLIGENCE.

HOPEFULLY INTACT AFTER THAT RATHER NASTY KNOCK ON THE HEAD. MAYBE A LITTLE *CONCUSSION* AT WORST.

OH, THAT'S NOT WHAT YOU MEAN, IS IT?

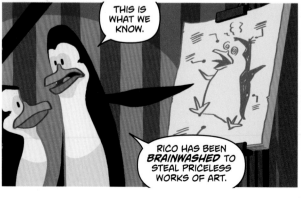

THIS IS WHAT WE KNOW.

RICO HAS BEEN *BRAINWASHED* TO STEAL PRICELESS WORKS OF ART.

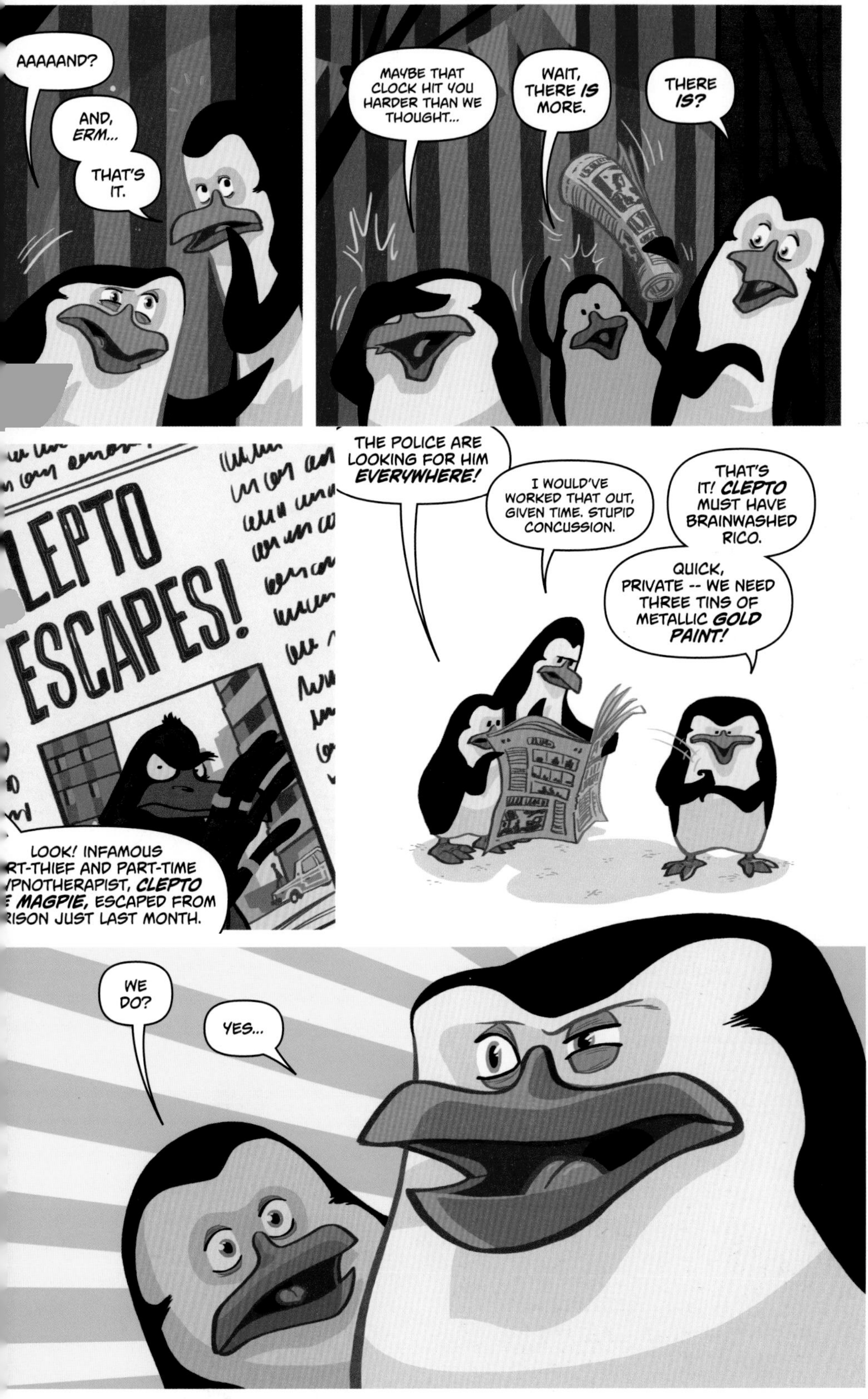
AAAAAND?
AND, ERM...
THAT'S IT.
MAYBE THAT CLOCK HIT YOU HARDER THAN WE THOUGHT...
WAIT, THERE IS MORE.
THERE IS?
LEPTO ESCAPES!
LOOK! INFAMOUS RT-THIEF AND PART-TIME YPNOTHERAPIST, CLEPTO E MAGPIE, ESCAPED FROM RISON JUST LAST MONTH.
THE POLICE ARE LOOKING FOR HIM EVERYWHERE!
I WOULD'VE WORKED THAT OUT, GIVEN TIME. STUPID CONCUSSION.
THAT'S IT! CLEPTO MUST HAVE BRAINWASHED RICO.
QUICK, PRIVATE -- WE NEED THREE TINS OF METALLIC GOLD PAINT!
WE DO?
YES...

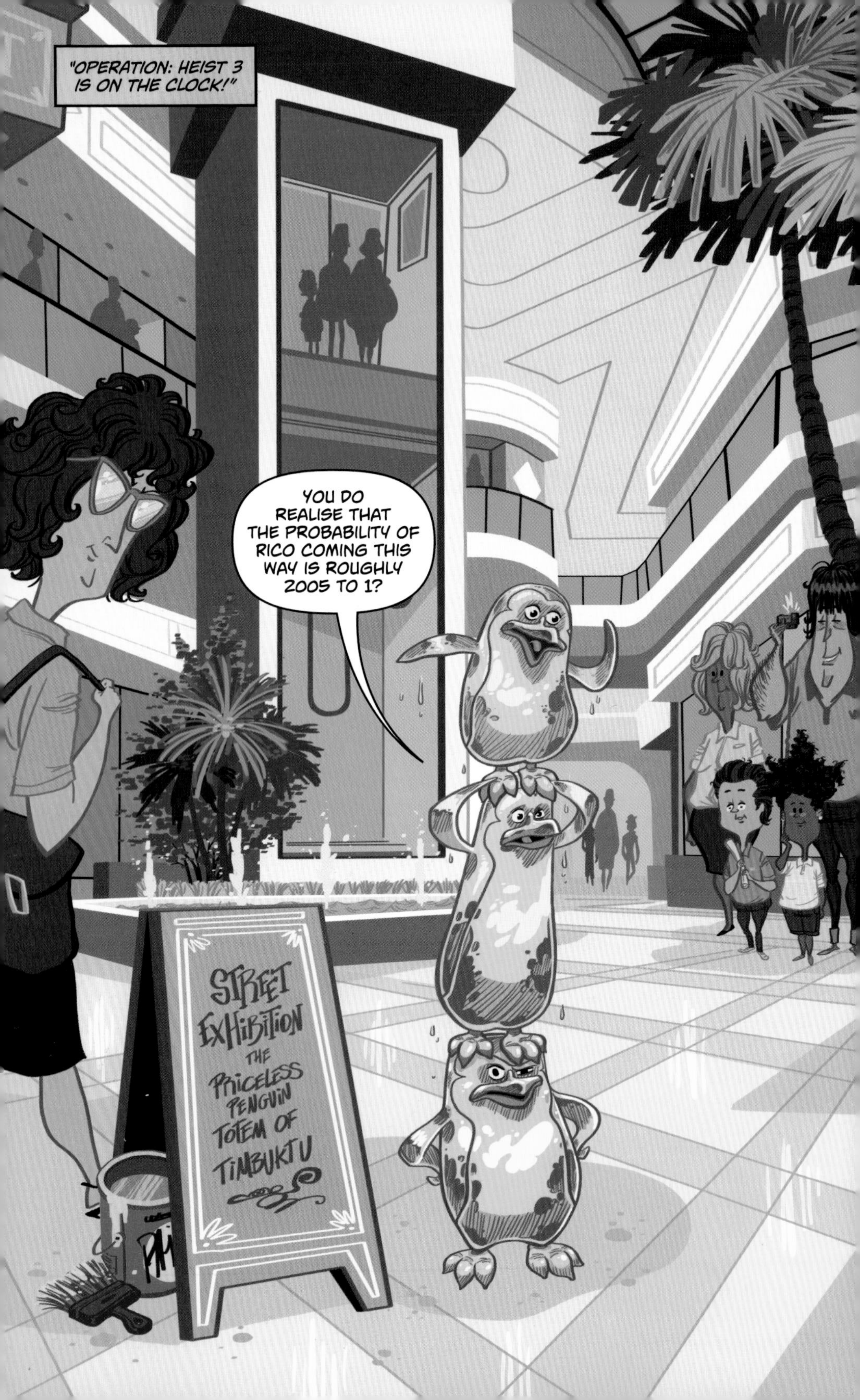
"OPERATION: HEIST 3 IS ON THE CLOCK!"
YOU DO REALISE THAT THE PROBABILITY OF RICO COMING THIS WAY IS ROUGHLY 2005 TO 1?
STREET EXHIBITION THE PRICELESS PENGUIN TOTEM OF TIMBUKTU

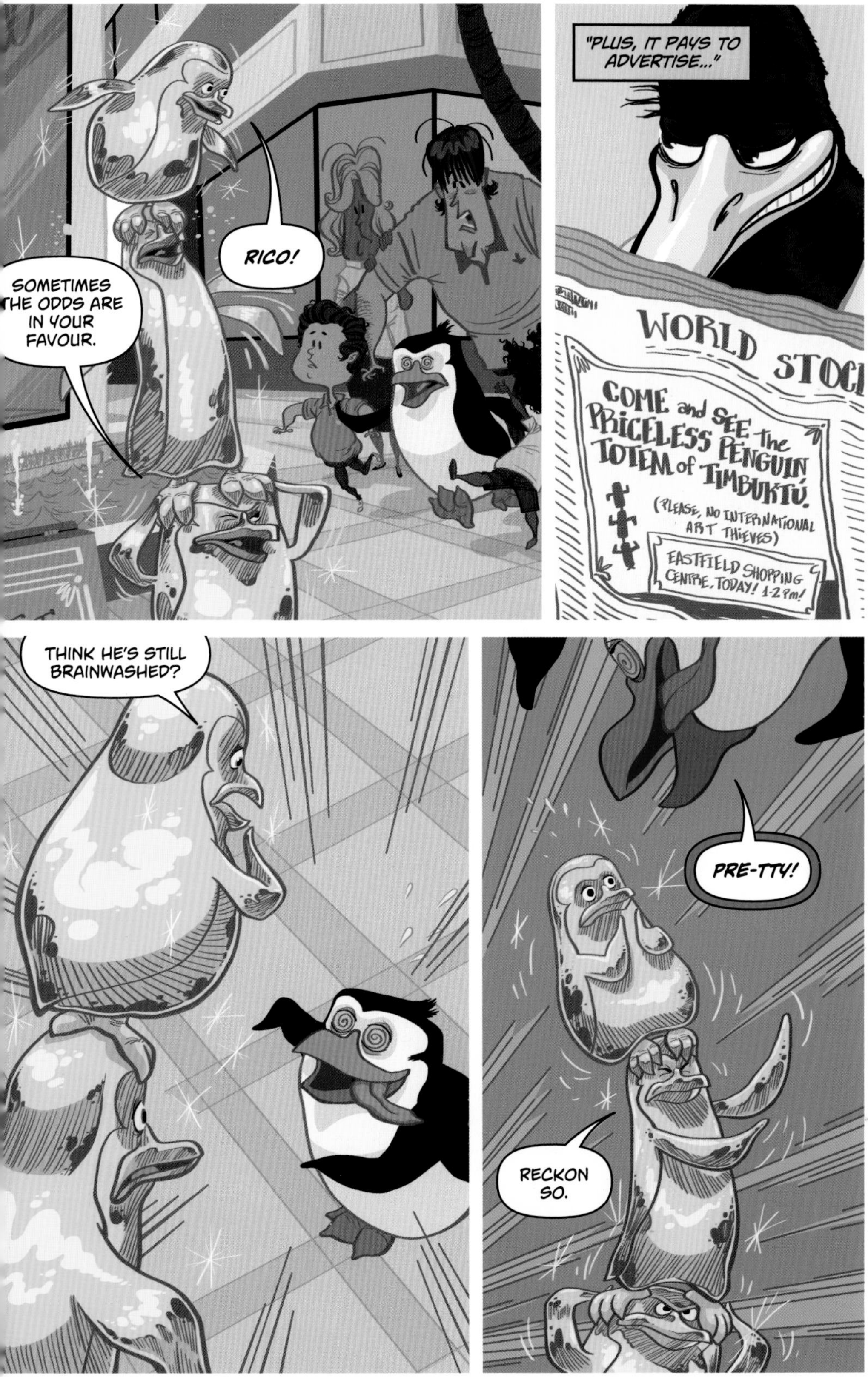
SOMETIMES THE ODDS ARE IN YOUR FAVOUR.
RICO!
"PLUS, IT PAYS TO ADVERTISE..."
WORLD STOC
COME and SEE the PRICELESS PENGUIN TOTEM of TIMBUKTÚ!
(PLEASE, NO INTERNATIONAL ART THIEVES)
EASTFIELD SHOPPING CENTRE, TODAY! 1-2 PM!
THINK HE'S STILL BRAINWASHED?
PRE-TTY!
RECKON SO.

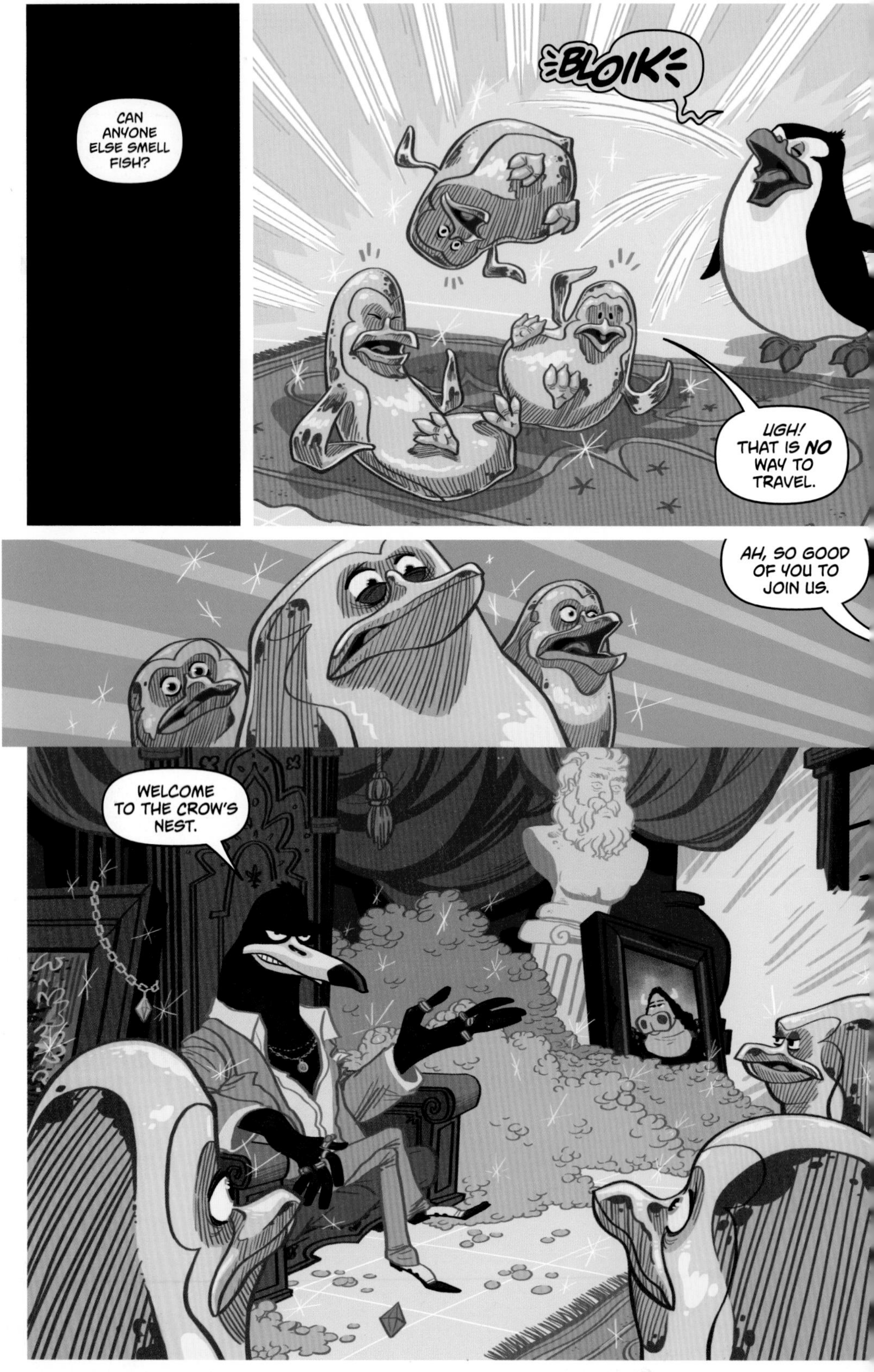
CAN ANYONE ELSE SMELL FISH?
BLOIK
UGH! THAT IS NO WAY TO TRAVEL.
AH, SO GOOD OF YOU TO JOIN US.
WELCOME TO THE CROW'S NEST.

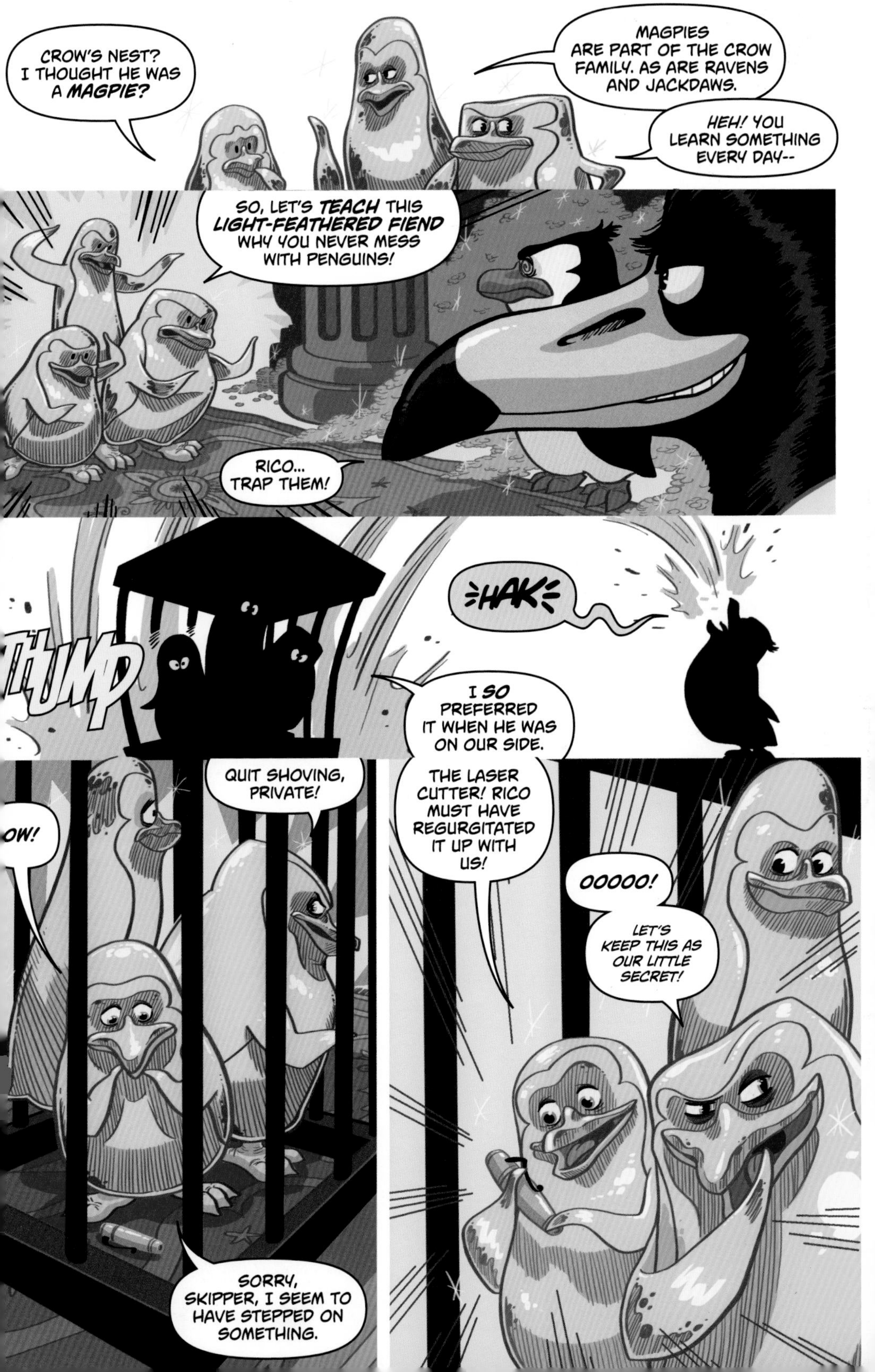

CROW'S NEST? I THOUGHT HE WAS A MAGPIE?
MAGPIES ARE PART OF THE CROW FAMILY. AS ARE RAVENS AND JACKDAWS.
HEH! YOU LEARN SOMETHING EVERY DAY--
SO, LET'S TEACH THIS LIGHT-FEATHERED FIEND WHY YOU NEVER MESS WITH PENGUINS!
RICO... TRAP THEM!
HAK
THUMP
I SO PREFERRED IT WHEN HE WAS ON OUR SIDE.
OW!
QUIT SHOVING, PRIVATE!
SORRY, SKIPPER, I SEEM TO HAVE STEPPED ON SOMETHING.
THE LASER CUTTER! RICO MUST HAVE REGURGITATED IT UP WITH US!
OOOOO!
LET'S KEEP THIS AS OUR LITTLE SECRET!

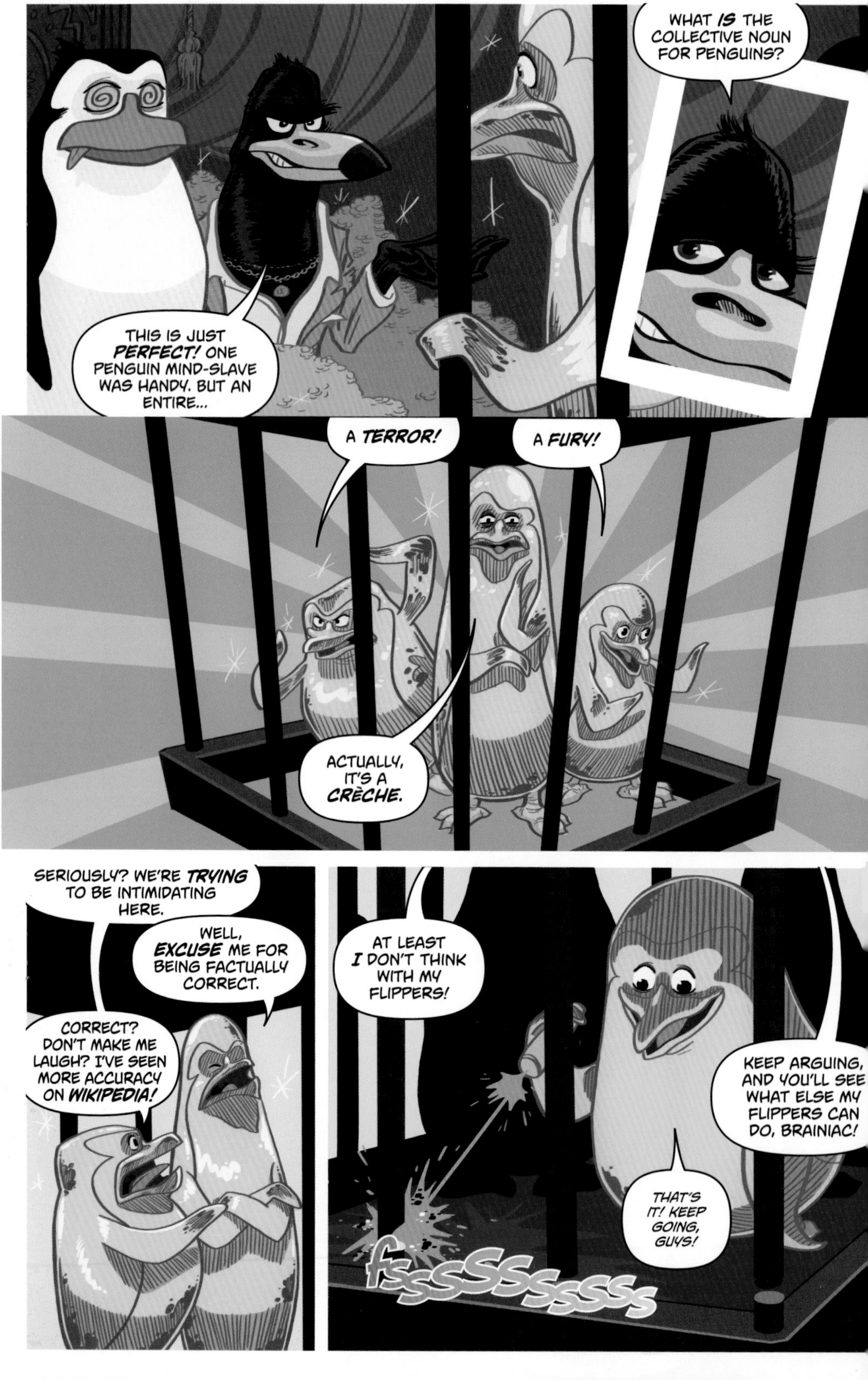
THIS IS JUST PERFECT! ONE PENGUIN MIND-SLAVE WAS HANDY. BUT AN ENTIRE...
WHAT IS THE COLLECTIVE NOUN FOR PENGUINS?
A TERROR!
A FURY!
ACTUALLY, IT'S A CRÈCHE.
SERIOUSLY? WE'RE TRYING TO BE INTIMIDATING HERE.
WELL, EXCUSE ME FOR BEING FACTUALLY CORRECT.
CORRECT? DON'T MAKE ME LAUGH? I'VE SEEN MORE ACCURACY ON WIKIPEDIA!
AT LEAST I DON'T THINK WITH MY FLIPPERS!
KEEP ARGUING, AND YOU'LL SEE WHAT ELSE MY FLIPPERS CAN DO, BRAINIAC!
THAT'S IT! KEEP GOING, GUYS!
fssSSSSsssss

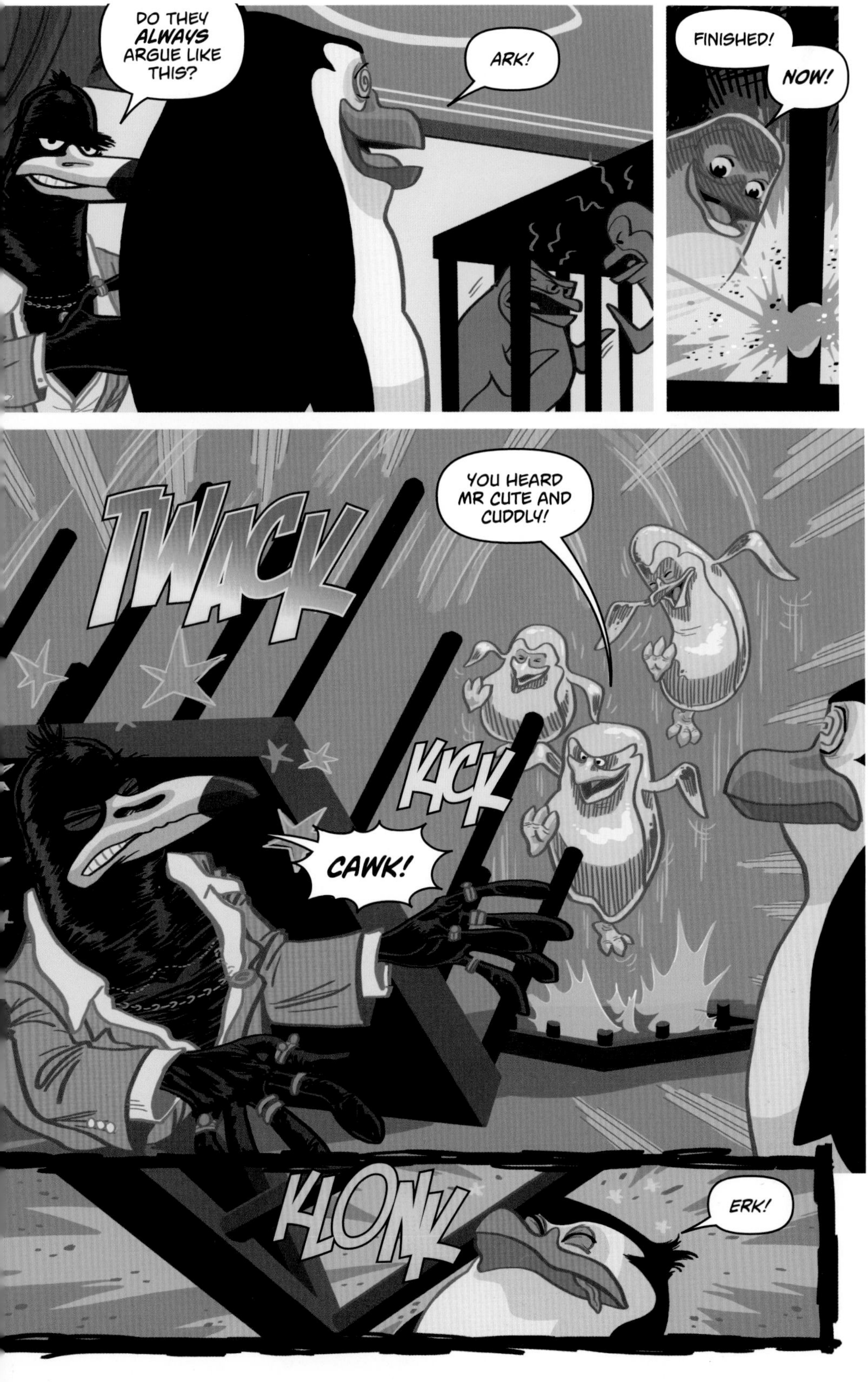

DO THEY ALWAYS ARGUE LIKE THIS?
ARK!
FINISHED!
NOW!
TWACK
YOU HEARD MR CUTE AND CUDDLY!
KICK
CAWK!
KLONK
ERK!

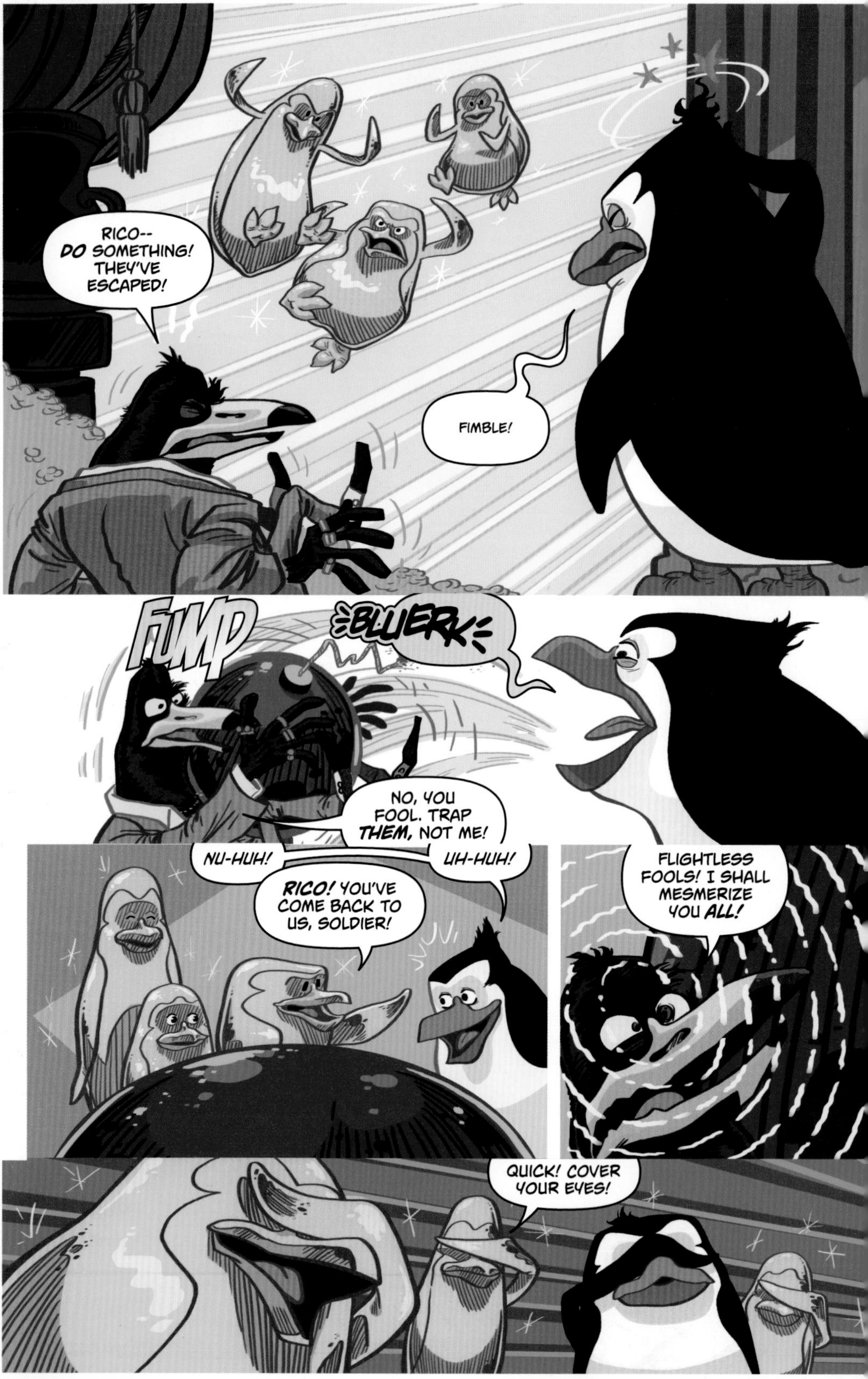
RICO--
DO SOMETHING! THEY'VE ESCAPED!
FIMBLE!
FUMP
BLUERK
NO, YOU FOOL. TRAP THEM, NOT ME!
NU-HUH!
UH-HUH!
RICO! YOU'VE COME BACK TO US, SOLDIER!
FLIGHTLESS FOOLS! I SHALL MESMERIZE YOU ALL!
QUICK! COVER YOUR EYES!

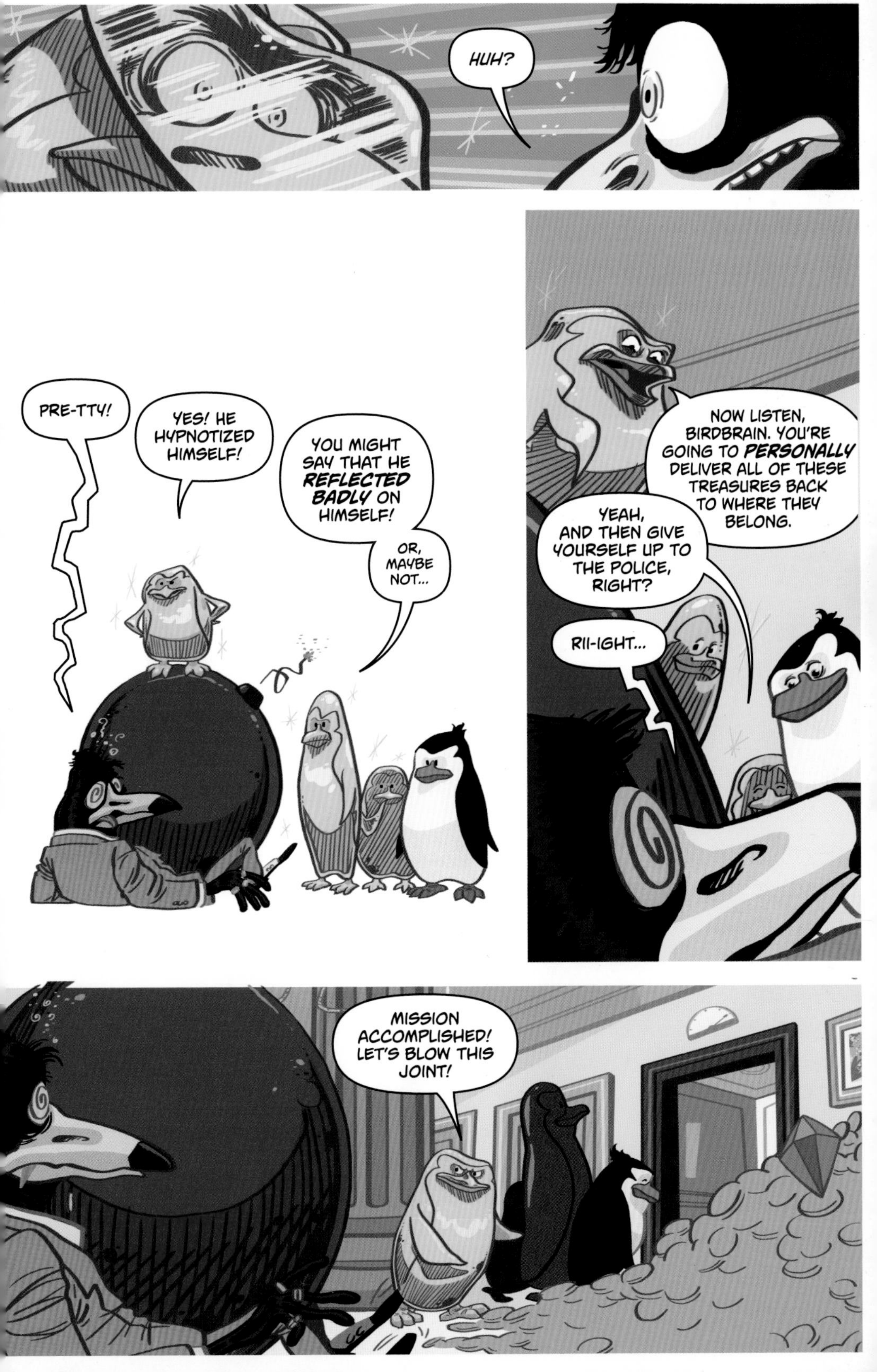
HUH?
PRE-TTY!
YES! HE HYPNOTIZED HIMSELF!
YOU MIGHT SAY THAT HE REFLECTED BADLY ON HIMSELF!
OR, MAYBE NOT...
NOW LISTEN, BIRDBRAIN. YOU'RE GOING TO PERSONALLY DELIVER ALL OF THESE TREASURES BACK TO WHERE THEY BELONG.
YEAH, AND THEN GIVE YOURSELF UP TO THE POLICE, RIGHT?
RII-IGHT...
MISSION ACCOMPLISHED! LET'S BLOW THIS JOINT!

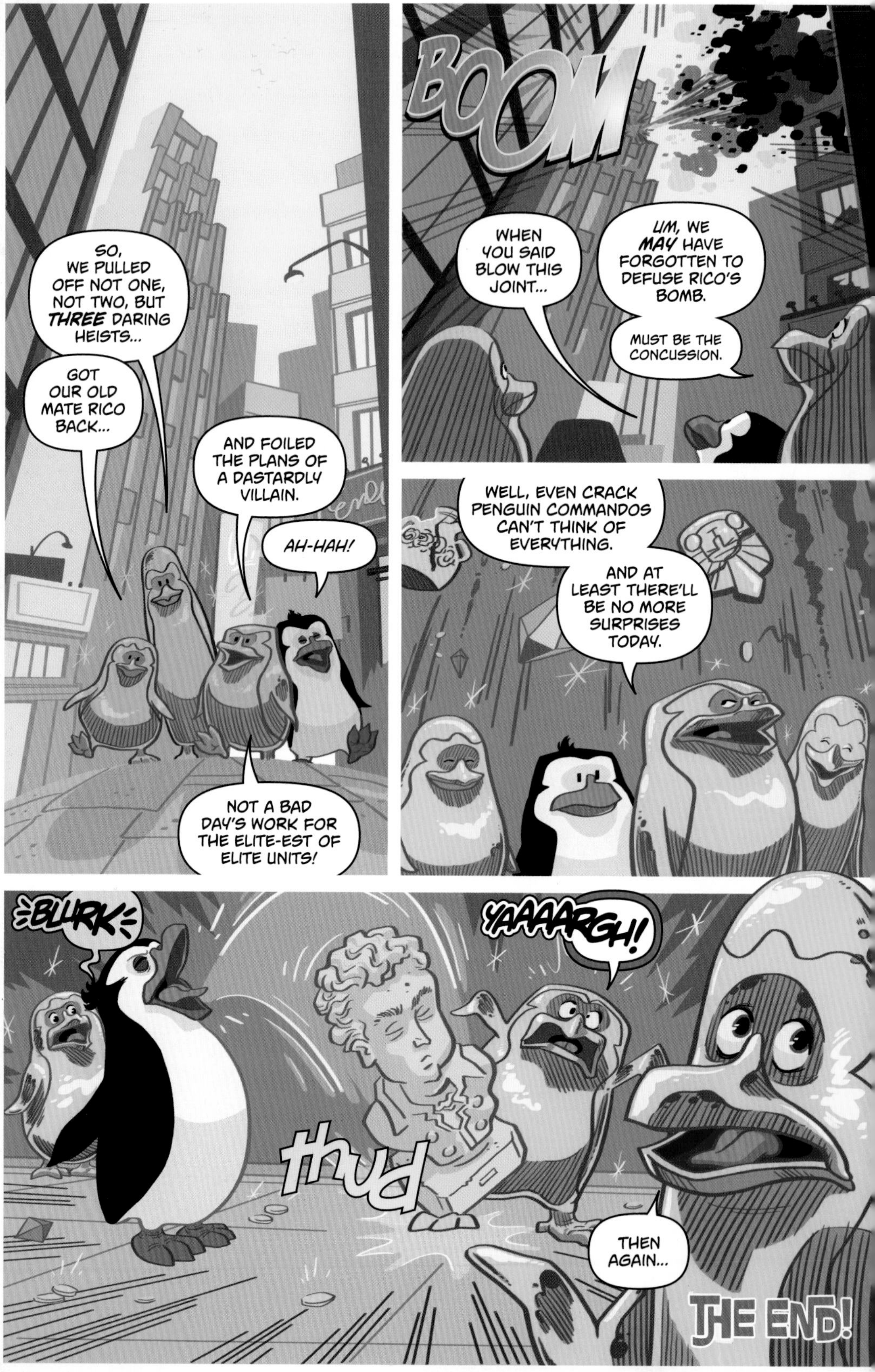
SO, WE PULLED OFF NOT ONE, NOT TWO, BUT THREE DARING HEISTS...
GOT OUR OLD MATE RICO BACK...
AND FOILED THE PLANS OF A DASTARDLY VILLAIN.
AH-HAH!
NOT A BAD DAY'S WORK FOR THE ELITE-EST OF ELITE UNITS!
BOOM
WHEN YOU SAID BLOW THIS JOINT...
UM, WE MAY HAVE FORGOTTEN TO DEFUSE RICO'S BOMB.
MUST BE THE CONCUSSION.
WELL, EVEN CRACK PENGUIN COMMANDOS CAN'T THINK OF EVERYTHING.
AND AT LEAST THERE'LL BE NO MORE SURPRISES TODAY.
BLURK
YAAAARGH!
thud
THEN AGAIN...
THE END!

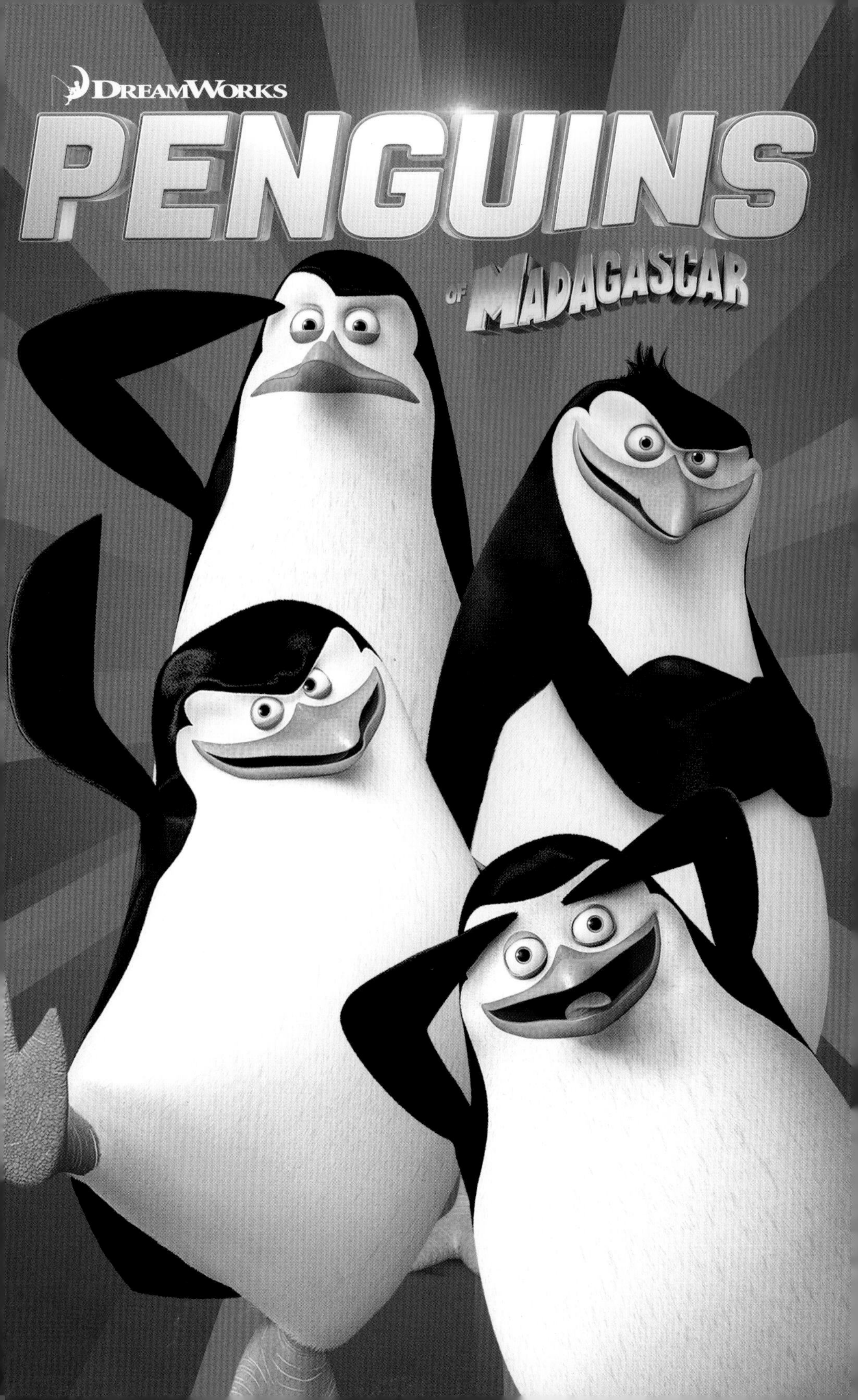
DreamWorks
PENGUINS
OF MADAGASCAR

PENGUIN
parade!

Penguins are the coooooolest birds on the planet! Find out all there is to know about our flippered friends!

Keeping Warm!

Penguins live on the Southern Hemisphere, especially in Antarctica. They're warm-blooded (just like us!), but some species spend as much as 75% of their lives at sea. To keep warm, their bodies are insulated by a layer of fat which keeps heat from escaping. They also have watertight feathers to keep them cosy underwater. And, Skipper's constant training would keep anyone warm!

Little and Large!

There are 17 different species of penguins. The biggest is the emperor penguin at 1.15m tall! An emperor penguin has yellow patches on each side of its head and a yellow patch on its breast.
The smallest penguin is the little blue penguin (also known as the fairy penguin). It's only 30cm tall and weighs less than 1kg! Awww!

Spot the Difference!

Can you spot the 6 differences between these flippered friends?

Spot the Difference answers: 1. Bird disappears from top right; 2. Penguin on right disappears; 3. Penguin's head-dress disappears; 4. Right penguin's neck detail changes; 5. Left penguin's neck color changes from green to yellow; 6. Right penguin's beak turns blue to orange.

Here are just a few of the many types of penguins!

Did you know?
Penguins don't drink water – they eat snow instead!

Speed Demon!
They can't fly, but penguins sure can swim! The torpedo shape of their body helps reduce drag in water, their webbed feet act like flippers and their paddle-like wings propel them up to speeds of 15mph! Of course, if you're Rico, you could regurgitate a small engine to make you go even faster!

Hide and Seek!
Their coloring might make them look a bit like waiters, but there's a good reason why penguins are black and white. Their dark backs help camouflage them when they are in the water. And when underwater predators look up at penguins, their white bellies are hard to see against the bright Antarctic skies! Cool!

Did you know?
Male penguins take care of their chicks.

EMPEROR PENGUIN 1.15m

KING PENGUIN 94cm

MAGELLANIC PENGUIN 74cm

LITTLE BLUE 30cm

DRAGONS GRAPHIC NOVELS

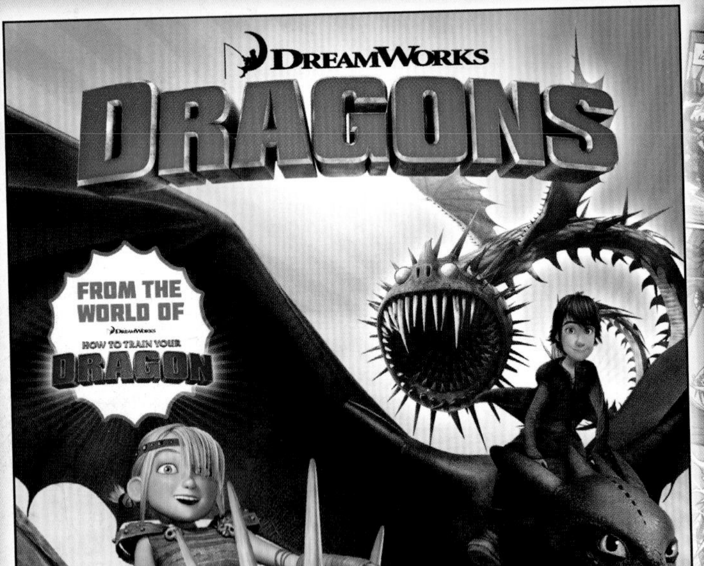
DREAMWORKS
DRAGONS
FROM THE WORLD OF
DREAMWORKS
HOW TO TRAIN YOUR
DRAGON
THE LEGEND OF RAGNAROK

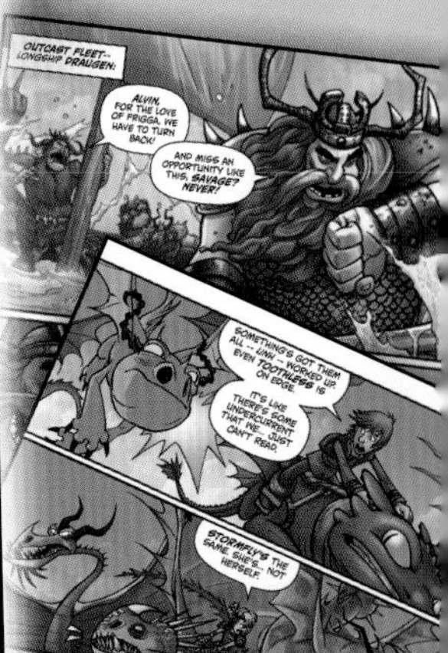
OUTCAST FLEET-- LONGSHIP DRAUGEN:
ALVIN, FOR THE LOVE OF FRIGGA, WE HAVE TO TURN BACK!
AND MISS AN OPPORTUNITY LIKE THIS, SAVAGE? NEVER!
SOMETHING'S GOT THEM ALL -- UHH -- WORKED UP. EVEN TOOTHLESS IS ON EDGE.
IT'S LIKE THERE'S SOME UNDERCURRENT THAT WE... JUST CAN'T READ.
STORMFLY'S THE SAME. SHE'S... NOT HERSELF.
YEEOW!
HUUUH!

VOLUME FIVE

OUT NOW $6.99

There is a scary prophecy in Berk that one day a huge monster will rise from the sea and the world will end... And then Hiccup and his friends encounter something huge and scary in the sea... Could this be the end of Berk? Plus a bonus story starring Astrid!